Praise for

"The characters are sharply drawn and ... standing out for their mix of oddball eccentricities and pluck ... OUR VERDICT: ✓GET IT." ~ *Kirkus Review*s (Recommended review)

"Kept me utterly hooked ... *Mail-Order Monsters* features well-developed themes of friendship, bravery, and honesty." ~ *Readers' Favorite (5 OUT OF 5 STARS)*

"Acevedo skillfully explores how loneliness can drive us to seek connection in the most unexpected places ... an exciting and immersive adventure that will capture reader's hearts from beginning to end." ~ *Midwest Book Review (VERDICT: RECOMMENDED)*

"The story is snappy and fresh, entertaining until the very last page ... Acevedo's ability to combine witty setups with deeper preadolescent issues is admirable." ~ *The BookLife Prize*

"Fun and fast-paced ... The themes of friendship and reconciliation are woven securely into the plot, and action in the final chapters just rockets the reader forward. Highly recommend this book for young boys in particular." ~ *Wisconsin Writers Association*

"This fast-paced, delightful adventure will have middle-grade readers (and up!) glued to the page as Marco attempts to solve his problems with a little help from some new friends. What could go wrong? Turns out—plenty!" ~ Valerie Biel, award-winning author of *Haven*

"Perfect for classrooms and read-aloud fun, *Mail-Order Monsters* is a thrilling, laugh-out-loud story about teamwork and the true meaning of friendship. Young readers will love the wild adventures, quirky creatures, and heartwarming moments that make this book an instant favorite!" ~ Christy Wopat, teacher and author of *Always Ours*

"A delightful, rollicking, action-packed tale of friendships—old and new—forgiveness, and the willingness to believe in the impossible.

A middle-grade must-read!" ~ Michelle Houts, author of *Winterfrost* and *Lucy's Lab*

"Clever, fun, fast-paced and filled with humor, kids will wish mail-order monsters were real in this delightfully relatable tale of about friendships and family." ~ Liza Wiemer, Sydney Taylor Notable Award-winning author of *The Assignment*

"What would you do if your best friend dumped you? Buy monsters, of course—and take them to school! Readers will enjoy discovering the creatures' capabilities, laughing at their school pranks, and cheering them on during the thrilling road race challenge." ~ Kristin Oakley, award-winning author of *The Death Particle* series

"This monstrously entertaining tale is a crash course in making mischief, surviving mayhem, and mending friendships." ~ Rochelle Melander, author of *Mightier Than the Sword: Rebels, Reformers, and Revolutionaries Who Changed the World through Writing*

"Acevedo's positive messages about friendship and family will be easy for young readers to understand. I can't wait to give a copy to my Godson." ~ Tracey S. Phillips, award-winning thriller author of *Forewarned*

"Buy this book, spend time with the mail-order monsters and you'll want to send away for a few of your own." ~ Laurie Scheer, writing mentor and Vice President of the Wisconsin Writers Association

"The title hooked me, but the hilarity and hijinks kept me turning the pages. Now I want my own mail-order monsters!" ~ Kerry Hansen, author of *Polterghost*

Mail-Order Monsters is a two-time award winner from the Society of Children's Book Writers and Illustrators:
Work of Outstanding Progress-Honor Winner—SCBWI Int'l
Most Promising Manuscript-Winner—SCBWI-IL

Mail-Order Monsters: Crash Course by Silvia Acevedo

Silvia Acevedo

THREE POINTS
PUBLISHING

Three Points Publishing

THREE POINTS
PUBLISHING

Three Points Publishing | P.O. Box 210862 | Milwaukee, WI 53221
Text copyright © 2025 by Silvia Acevedo | SilviaAcevedo.com
Illustrations copyright © 2025 by Jeff Miracola | JeffMiracola.com

Summary: A 10-year-old boy desperate for a new best friend orders monsters from an ad in the back of an old comic book.

All rights reserved. No part of this publication may be reproduced, distributed, or transmitted in any form or by any means, including photocopying, recording, or other electronic or mechanical methods, without the express, prior, written permission of the publisher, except as permitted by U.S. copyright law. For permission requests, contact Three Points Publishing at info@threepointspublishing.com. No part of this work was created using generative AI.

The story, names, characters, and incidents portrayed in this production are fictitious. No identification with actual persons (living or deceased), places, buildings, and products is intended or should be inferred.

ISBN 978-1-950150-01-4 (pbk) | ISBN 978-1-950150-02-1 (EPUB)
First Edition | Printed in the United States of America

Library of Congress Control Number: 2025903684

For Eliza,
who asks me to check for monsters under the bed.
May she someday love these monster friends.

Chapter 1
The Ad

Marco Torres held scissors poised inches over a photograph. The fact that he had a *printed* photo was Tinker's doing. All of Marco's photos were in his phone, where they belonged, saving the Earth by saving ink. But Tinker had printed this one so they'd both have a physical copy. In the pic, they stood side by side, arms draped over each others' shoulders. Smiling and laughing.

Marco frowned. Had the pic been in his phone, he could edit out his ex-best friend with a few taps. But this real-life photo? Not so easy. He positioned the blades on either side of the shiny photo paper, along Tinker's polo shirt, ready to slice him out, but Marco's head kept saying *mala idea, bad idea.* He held the scissors a long time, wanting to be certain. His fingers got sweaty.

After a few minutes, he folded the pic in half, bending Tinker out of sight, and looked through his bedroom window to the blackness outside. He had hours to go until the start of the second week of fifth grade. And this week promised to be worse than the first. He returned his gaze to his room and set his scissors to cut into his pop's vintage comic book. A few weeks ago, an unbelievable advertisement on the last page caught his attention with a big promise:

*Order your very own monsters!
Creepy or crawly,
hairy or scary,
fearsome or cheersome,
you'll love your new monster pals!
They're guaranteed to become your favorite sidekicks. Order now!*

Marco wished he was in a spot where he didn't *need* a new favorite sidekick, but sometimes a person had to stick up for themself. Even if it felt dumb as rocks. *Really, my man? Monsters?* he asked himself. *Que locura,* like Papi says. *What craziness. How desperate am I?*

He cut around the ad. At each corner, pivoting his scissors, he ignored the logic telling him that monsters don't exist, that toys can't be best friends, and that an order form from a weird ad in a super old comic book must be, for sure, expired. When he made the final snip, he said out loud, as if talking to the ad, that he didn't really *need* any mail-order monsters as friends.

Only, deep down, he felt that last bit wasn't quite, exactly, 100 percent true.

Chapter 2

The Mailbox and the Microwave

After getting dressed and eating breakfast, Marco hoofed over to the post office. Standing in front of an ancient blue mailbox, he fed it the envelope containing his order form and payment. The dented metal box sucked it in with a *shooop*.

This is stupid, and snail-mailing an order form is an extra scoop of stupid on top. He pressed the heel of his hands against his overtired eyes and asked out loud, "Who still does this?"

A cough from behind made him turn to see a giant of a man with a scraggly, gray beard, wearing a scuffed motorcycle jacket.

"Oh. Sorry." Marco stepped out of the way.

Biker Guy held an envelope in a hand with huge knuckles and as many scars as a cutting board. The outside of the envelope was embellished with curly, confident handwriting. No one in fifth grade could write that well. Biker Guy dropped his envelope into the box and turned back. "Need something?" he asked. A fleck of spit landed in his beard.

Marco stared at the spit and answered, "For magic to exist in our everyday world." He hadn't meant to say it. It just sort of slipped out. Another scoop of stupid for today.

Biker Guy stared a beat before shrugging off his jacket and lifting the sleeve of his T-shirt to reveal a wizard tattoo that waved its wand with each bicep flex. "Don't worry, kid. It does."

Marco nodded and turned away before he could say anything else out of whack.

• • • ● ● • ● ● • • •

As he balance-walked on the curb on his way to school, he questioned every aspect of the monster ad. Cash only, standard for scammers. And there was the ridiculously low price of one dollar per monster, but then Marco remembered that a dollar was worth more back when the ad was made, maybe fifty years ago? His dad had said the comics were old back when he got them. *And the ad did limit orders to three monsters each, so the company can't be looking to make big money, right?* There was also no web address for the company, which Marco didn't like until he remembered the internet didn't exist back then.

All that weirdness aside, Marco really wanted to believe the ad.

He rounded the corner of Cesar Chavez Drive and Mitchell Street and saw a dozen kids running into Gabriel García Márquez K-8, his red brick neighborhood school on Milwaukee's south side. He'd barely make it in time. He dashed past the heavy, wooden doors just as the warning bell rang. Sprinting down the halls, he spotted new artwork taped around open cubbies—*ooh, I'll check that out later.* He slammed into his class's open doorway, skittered into the room, and slid into his desk. The final bell rang. *Whew.*

Mrs. Kroppert, his teacher, frowned. Marco was glad she didn't say anything because, when she was mad, her words went short like a dog barking at rabbits. Most times, her voice just droned, like the whirr of a microwave. *Reeerrrr, reeerrrr.* Marco knew it wasn't nice to imagine people as pets or appliances, but he couldn't help what his brain did by itself.

As she started her lesson on misplaced commas, Marco looked at his ex-best friend, Tinker, sitting to his right in the next column of seats. Tink wore grey jeans and a blue T-shirt. They looked ocean-y, like waves crashing against brown sand and black rocks, his skin and tiny, tight curls. *Might as well have an ocean between us,* Marco thought. *That argument. The things we said. The way we acted.* He decided not to think about it anymore or his chest would tighten.

"Marco," came a whisper behind him and to the right, just behind Tinker. He ignored it.

"Marciano." Same stupid voice.

"MARTIAN!"

Marco whipped around to glare at Knox Cariño, the only person who called him *marciano*—"Martian" in English. Knox had been saying it a lot lately, even though they were supposedly friends. But their friendship was unraveling like frayed rope.

"What?" Marco hissed.

"Did ya stick your finger in a light socket, loser?"

Marco replied by narrowing his eyes, then turning to see his ghosted reflection in the room's back windows. Sure enough, his normally messy brown hair spiked in all directions, like he'd set a porcupine on his head. He scanned his memory and couldn't picture himself combing his hair that morning. *Probably didn't. Too busy cutting out ads for monsters.*

"Oooooh, you're in trouuuuuuuble," someone sang.

Marco swiveled in his chair and went wide-eyed at Mrs. Kroppert clomping his way. The hollows of her cheeks, almost blue, got bigger and clearer as she got closer. *Frightening.* She slapped her bony hands onto his desk.

"First late," she accused, "and now disrupting my class?"

Marco wanted to point out that wasn't late, just *nearly* so. But with her, he never stood a chance, not since the first day of school when Knox clucked like a chicken, over and over again, apparently hoping to rattle the class. Every time Mrs. Kroppert turned around, Knox turned to look at him. So naturally, she thought *Marco* was to blame. *And everyone knows how first impressions go. Once a teacher thinks you're a bad egg, you're cooked.*

"Mr. Torres."

Uh oh. Her voice going bark-like. Building up steam for a public scolding. It *was* the end of the world.

"Do you think. I stand up here talking. Because I need the practice?" She straighted. "I hope you can pay attention now. Because I promise you. This lesson. Will be. On the quiz tomorrow." She skewered him with a final glare before heading back to the front of the room.

Marco heard a chuckle to his right and caught Tinker laughing into his cupped hand. He didn't know if Tink was laughing *at* him or *with* him, but he wasn't going to react. The hardest part about giving someone the silent treatment, he decided, was that you actually had to be silent. Like, ignore them, even if they *were* your best friend just two weeks ago and even if the whole thing *was* kinda funny. But Marco guessed you really couldn't laugh with an *ex*-best friend.

Chapter 3
Stripes and Likes

At lunch, Marco plunked down next to Maite. *Finally, some good luck.* Unfortunately, Tinker sat at her other side. Across were her twin brother, Knox, and Rosita, the youngest Cariño. He and Tinker kept the silence thick between them, and Knox hid his mean streak. Marco used to love this lunch group. Now? *Ay de mí. Not so much.* But it seemed nobody wanted to move tables. Marco certainly didn't want to start someplace new.

"Mac-n-cheese," he said while nodding at Maite's plate. "Smart choice."

"Pizza," she answered. "So, so foolish."

Rosita pulled a rainbow-striped spinning top from a pocket and flicked it onto the table. "Marco," she chirped, "today at recess, I'm working on penny drops." She waved her hands to mimic swinging by the knees on a low bar, releasing into a back flip, and landing right side up.

"Ooh, those are tough," Marco said, "but you'll land 'em."

Her face split into a smile. She was missing baby teeth. Her ponytails were a little off, one shock of light brown hair higher than the other. And her purple T-shirt with pink horses in no way matched her green jeans. Marco liked that.

"What about you two?" Maite asked, looking at him and Tinker in turn. Marco caught a sugary sweet scent, maybe from the movement of her hair. He was suddenly struck, again, by how different she was from her twin. He learned years ago that fraternal twins come from different eggs, so even though they're born together, they don't look any more alike than other siblings. Maite had golden brown hair that exactly matched her eyes. Knox had blonde—almost white—hair and eyes so dark they were nearly black. Marco realized those dark eyes were staring back with enough force to make his face cave from the pressure.

He looked away.

"Ugh, when are you and Tink going to start talking again?"

It's not just Tink and me who've got problems, Marco thought.

"Don't worry, MaiMai. They'll make up." Rosita pulled a deck of animal cards out of her back pocket and dealt before anyone could say no. "Let's play Go Fish."

As Marco grouped sea stars, jellyfish, and octopi, he noticed the otherwise deafening silence at his table. He missed being young enough that friend-fights lasted just minutes and games fixed everything.

· · · · ● · ● · · ·

After recess—which they spent apart because ex-friends don't play together and neither does a bully—his day got worse. He didn't expected it because Art is his favorite class.

"Find your vejigante mask," Ms. Mira called as students filed in. "Please put on the smock draped over your chair and let's get started."

Marco spotted his mask quickly. In the final minute of the previous class, when other kids had laid the papier-mâché masks out to harden, he wrote "Marco" across his because it looked sad and gray, and he didn't want it to feel lonely. But it wasn't alone. Tinker's mask rested next to it, as did two more across the table. Ms. Mira always arranged friends next to each other because she thought "art should be social, a gift to the whole community."

Hpmf. Now's def not the best time for community with Tink. Marco searched for empty chairs, but didn't spot any, so he sat. At least Knox was waaaay off in the far corner.

Looking at his unfinished, handmade vejigante mask, he pictured the slick, store-bought one he'd bought during his last visit to Puerto Rico. Carnival street performers danced in frilly costumes or wore these amazingly colorful masks with horns that looked like dragon heads. Most of his classmates were Latino, and he heard their excitement at making vejigantes, a welcome change from making more capotain hats—the brimmed hats the Pilgrims wore with flat tops and buckles. His class had made more of those than made sense.

"Next to each mask is an egg carton," Ms. Mira said. Her black, curly hair was stacked high on her head, and Marco thought her red lips matched her personality. "You'll find paint and clean brushes at center table. Pour whatever colors you'd like into each well, but don't mix them unless you're sure you don't want the original colors. There's no way to un-mix them later."

The class laughed. Marco smiled, grateful he got to paint in school. The past two weeks he'd spent evenings alone in his room, painting his remote control truck, one of two he'd bought in August with money from summer chores. He kept the blue one and gave the green one to Tink. *Too bad we only had a couple weeks with them before our argument.* In that short time, they walked everywhere with them, testing different surfaces, even taping his phone onto one to shoot video. Now the phone was a toxic reminder of a friendship gone bad. He hadn't used it since.

Marco knew Tinker planned to modify his RC truck by souping up the engine, making it faster, so Marco worked to make his *look* faster. He chose a shark. *If we were still friends, Tink could amp up both our trucks, and I could paint cogs and gears on his. But now? Pues, nada. Nope.* Painting alone, especially painting a shark, a predator, made him more and more angry. He used sandpaper to roughen the truck's smooth surface so it could grip paint. He slapped down grey primer, then slashed white triangles for the shark's face and fins. He stabbed a brush coated in yellow along its snout to make jagged, pointy teeth. *It's easy to paint teeth when you're mad.*

But he wasn't angry now. How could he be, painting a carnival mask? He poured black, blue, red, and yellow into each well. No blending, so the colors would be vibrant, loud enough for him to dance in. He grabbed a brush, dipped it in blue, and ran the bristles along a horn for a stripe. It reminded him of the monster ad. "Pick your stripes and likes," meaning, pick your favorites. Three stood out, so he picked them without another thought.

"When you've finished with one color," Ms. Mira said, "set the brush at center table and grab another loaded with your new color so we don't have to wash brushes after each use."

Marco glanced over to ensure Knox was where he'd last seen him. *Yep. Good.* Knox's mask was black with red stripes racing up the horns. It didn't vibe happiness. It felt sinister.

Marco turned back to his own mask and imagined himself dancing in the street, his mask magically transforming him into a dragon so big the street could barely hold him. He'd weave his scaly, muscled body high over the crowds, expanding his immense wings. The crowd would *oooooh* and *aaaaah*. No one would dare stand in his way because a bad move could get them blasted with fire.

Suddenly the crowd would part as Knox walked onto the street. Marco imagined himself swaying his terrifying dragon head, his long horns taking up space and sending an unmistakable message: *Nobody better mess with me.* Knox was a big kid, tall and built like a brick wall, but there, on the street, he seemed to shrink. His clothes, all black with red stripes, didn't seem so scary anymore. Marco smiled to himself before the tropical paradise he imagined tumbled away.

Back in the reality of art class, Marco decided to paint ears on his mask. He reached for a brush. But he never connected. A hard, awful push against his back launched his mask from his hand. Marco watched in horror as one of his best art projects tumbled onto the table and spun across. He saw, as if in slow motion, others lift their masks to safety. A yell formed in his throat as his own mask collided with egg cartons and pitched toward the table's far end.

Marco threw himself toward it. His smock was so coated with paint that he slid across the table. Egg cartons flew outward and spewed paint everywhere. Marco's torso tipped over the table's edge. Before he hit the ground, he caught a glimpse of his mask balanced on Tinker's foot and Tinker's hand reaching for it. But nothing could rescue Marco from his own momentum. His head hit the floor. He heard and felt his teeth clack. The rest of him plopped down, along with everything else that had been on the table. For a second, he saw stars.

"My clothes!" shouted a girl. Her voice sounded muffled, like he was hearing it through paint. Ms. Mira ran over while kids scrambled to sinks and jostled for space. She put a hand on his shoulder to keep him still and asked more than once if he was okay.

Marco couldn't be sure who pushed him, but he saw Knox walking away toward a sink, laughing so loud it rung through the room.

Tink's face hovered into view. He raised the mask he'd managed to rescue.

Chapter 4

Monsters Delivered

After Tink rescued his vejigante, he set the mask on the table and kept on painting. Marco couldn't understand why he'd done it. And, he wondered if Knox would say anything. He didn't know why he expected him to apologize, to say he hadn't meant to shove him hard enough for his mask to fly, or that he hadn't meant to shove at all, hadn't meant to hurt him, hadn't meant to be mean, hadn't meant to bully. But Knox didn't apologize. Instead, the big lug shoulder-checked him later in the hall. So Marco spent the remainder of the day picturing himself with huge, hulking monsters beside him, making everything else not matter. He held that thought the next *four days* until Friday afternoon finally rolled in, bringing with it the sweet promise of a weekend away from ex-friends and frenemies.

Tengo un montón en que pensar, Marco thought and decided he'd do that ton of thinking at home, creating art, where his best ideas bubbled up. When Friday's final bell rang, he speed-walked through the halls, the fastest he could go without running, and spilled out of school with the rest of the crowd into glaring September sunlight. He shot off at a run. When he plunged into his front entry, he found his pop on the sofa, waiting for him.

"Hola, hijo. Primero, un abrazo. Entonces quiero preguntarte algo."

Marco crossed over to him and wrapped his arms around his stubbly neck for the requested hug, while trying to read his face, not knowing what question he might possibly have.

"Hijo, tu mamá pasó una hora entera limpiando tu cuarto. Hay que limpiarlo tú mismo."

Oh. Yikes. He knew he had to clean his own room. Why would his mom go in there? "¿Por qué entró-?"

"Porque tenía que dejarte algo. Pero tu cuarto estaba hecho un revolú, hijo, y apestaba. Debes lavar tu propia ropa."

Oh, that's why she went in, dropping something off. And yeah, sometimes he let his dirty clothes pile up. *Stupid chores. It's hard to remember everything everyone wants done.* Parents, teachers, friends. It was a lot.

He scrunched his face. "¿Dónde está Mami?"

"La cocina." His pop nodded toward the kitchen, answering where she was.

"¡Ajá! Aquí éstas," his mom said when Marco pushed through the kitchen's swinging door. She stopped grinding spices in the pilón to face him. "¿Qué piensas?"

"Sorry, Mami, I'll finish with my clothes."

"En español, por favor." *Spanish, please.*

"Disculpa, Mami. Terminaré yo mismo con la ropa." Marco was pretty sure he said it right. He spoke a lot more English at school than Spanish at home, so there were a ton of words he didn't know en español. But his Spanglish was excellent.

"Llegó un paquete. Está en tu cuarto."

A package arrived? And it's in my room? He stood frozen on the spot for what seemed like a full minute. But it couldn't have been more than a few seconds because his mom didn't react in any weird way. When Marco snapped out of it, he nodded thanks, turned, and bounded up the stairs toward his room. When he pushed open his door, all logical thought whooshed out of his head. *Whew! It does stink in here! A dumpster couldn't smell this bad.* But! There! Right on his bed lay a package wrapped in brown paper and tied with white string. Next to his address, stickers had been slapped that read "Fragile" and "MOM Co."

The Mail-Order Monsters Company. Marco thought. *Fenomenal.* He couldn't believe the package had come only five days after he'd snail-mailed his order, but it had gone to an in-state address—468 Scary Lane, Monsterville, Wisconsin. Maybe in-state mail traveled faster. Still, the advertisement said to expect delivery in six to eight weeks, so this was lightning fast, especially since Marco half expected the company to be out of business. *Whadayaknow, MOM Co. is still in action.*

The package really did smell, but he didn't much care. The delivery driver could have frosted the packaged with rotten eggs for all he cared. What mattered was what was inside. Monsters. Supposedly. He desperately hoped MOM Co. hadn't filled it with some worthless plastic junk on hand instead—what if they'd run out of monsters? What were the chances the company had real monsters to ship out?

The only way to know was to unwrap the package. He steeled himself, preparing, in case it didn't hold what he was hoping for. He tamped down his emotions *porque estoy en necesidad*, he admitted, and being in need is no small thing. And what he needed was new besties, big, burly friends to make Tinker jealous and force Knox out of reach and keep himself from feeling so alone. He felt his heart pinch, like it was making itself small, folding up to protect itself.

But Marco decided to straighten his back. Stand tall. Make peace with whatever was in there and be grateful for anything he got from an ad that was decades old. *Let's do this.*

He grabbed the same scissors he used days ago to cut out the monster ad and oh-so-carefully slit the tape. He cut the string, slit the paper, and pulled it apart to reveal a wooden box, like a crate with etchings of more Mom Co. and Fragile, but also a burned-on image of a toothy, three-eyed monster. And claw marks. Clear claw marks. Marco sucked in a breath, slid the lid open, and reached in. Pulling out a crinkly wad of yellow tissue paper and holding it high, he saw... he realized... the monsters he'd been so desperately hoping for were...

three

rubbery

toys.

Marco stared at them, disbelieving, before plucking them from their paper nest. He couldn't process what he was seeing. All three of those tiny figurines fit into one hand.

He felt a spike of pain in the middle of his chest. *This* was his great rescue party? *These* tiny, puny, lifeless toys were his new best friends? *They're just toys. Not living monsters. Just ... toys. And they stink.*

A thought struck him. *What ... exactly ... did I ... expect? I cut and mailed an ad for monsters, and that's bogus, right? Monsters are a joke? And the package itself is small, so why didn't I realize right away when I walked in here that there couldn't be real monsters inside? Did the smell throw me off? Because this box is a six-inch square. No real monsters could fit unless they're...simplemente...jugetes. Mere toys. Debería haberlo sabido. I should have known.*

The pain in his chest pushed its way up. Squeezed his throat. Swelled behind his eyes. Threatened to explode. Before Marco could stop it, tears spilled down his cheeks. He stared at the junk he was sent and let his stupid angry tears flow. He couldn't believe he fell for it. He thanked los cielos that he hadn't told anyone he'd ordered monsters. How humiliating would that have been? *How could I have been so naive, tan simplón?*

He stared at them, wanting to burn into his memory exactly what ripoffs look like. Each figure was about three inches tall. They looked like the drawings on the order form—fairly realistic, even lifelike, as far as toys go. They reminded him of the plastic dinosaurs he got at the natural history museum: put a dollar into the machine and watch it cast a model from a mold. But the coating on the monsters felt less rigid, a little squishy, kind of rubbery. He didn't want to get too curious about them, but he couldn't resist pushing his finger into one's belly. The indent held for a second before returning to form like the super stretchy "Stretch Armstrong" action figure Papi had, passed down from his own pop. Kids in the 1970s supposedly played tug of war with them. The one in the attic looked like it had been chewed by a dog.

Marco focused again on the figures.

One was skinny with mismatched patterns across its body. Zebra stripes streaked across its neck on up. Leopard spots dotted its chest and stomach. One arm flaunted black and white checkers. The other, leaves and bark. One leg seemed made of stacked bricks. The other churned with a foaming, raging sea. Somehow, though, its black-beaded eyes looked friendly.

The second monster was red and partly-hairy-partly-smooth like a gorilla. Unlike a gorilla, though, this monster had furry tentacles crowning its head. Marco wondered, if the monster were real, would its tentacles sway? Sense surroundings? Grab things? Or maybe they'd be expressive, like a cat's tail? He felt a shiver run up his spine. If this monster been real and about six feet taller, it would've been menacing enough to scare a big kid like Knox and any other bully that might come his way.

The third monster had eyes on stalks and splotchy green skin. It sported yellow, leathery fringes that flapped from its armpits and a feathery mane, also yellow, that ran from the top of its head to its butt. This was the only monster with a mane.

Maybe that's why it smelled so ... barnyard. Marco lifted it to his nose and gagged. *Ugh.* This monster smelled like filthy hay—and putrid fruit—and rotten cheese—and unwashed-for-a-month, standing-up-by-themselves sweat socks. Marco immediately dropped it and brought his hands to his nose. They reeked.

So these were the monsters—*toys*—he'd ordered. *One's weird, another's stinky, and only one looks scary. What a total letdown.* Marco washed the funk off his hands and hoped his parents would be understanding that he'd blown money on junk that stunk up his room. They sometimes gave him odd jobs around the house specifically to earn money and buy stuff on his own, and, probably, he figured, to learn lessons about spending.

He dropped the toys in their box and was about to take them to the garbage when he spotted a letter within. He hadn't noticed before. He snagged it and read:

"Congratulations! Your Mail-Order Monsters are HERE! You'll have loads of laughs and terrific times—once you BRING THEM TO LIFE!"

Wuuut? He read on.

"Here's what you'll need to do. Have faith, follow these directions, and your miniature monsters will grow overnight.

Take a BUBBLE BATH with your monsters. Play in the water while you TALK to them. GAB your guts out. SPILL your precious secrets. SHARE your hopes and dreams. TELL the truth. Let them know the REAL YOU and what you hope for in a monster friend."

Marco's vision suddenly dolly zoomed, like in movies, when the camera focuses on someone but their background gets farther away. Just like that, his bedroom fell waaay back while the letter got bigger. *Does this mean what I think it means? Is-is this real?* He barely dared to believe and was struck by that last bit. What *did* he hope for in a monster friend? He thought he knew, but telling it to them—out loud—might sharpen his fuzzy focus. He kept reading.

"When an hour has passed, that mucky, muddy water will be dirty with the truth and the residue of at least one of your days. It will hold a bit of you and your life.

Pluck out your pocket-sized pals and drain the tub. (Don't let your monster friends go down the drain or you'll be sorry.) Then, to add even more spice to their makeup, wrap them in the same clothes you've worn that day.

Don't wipe away any soap scum that stays behind. Leave your wrapped monsters in the tub overnight.

If you follow these directions—and have faith—your monsters will CHANGE.

Forming friends forever,

MOM Co."

Marco lowered the letter from under his nose. *Those were the strangest directions I've ever read. If this is part of a long con, a sick way to trick kids and stretch out their humiliation, well, it's cruel.*

Marco almost didn't want to do it. *How many kids like me have been made fools of by following this advice?* But he couldn't *not* do it. He'd trust MOM Co. just a little bit more. No matter how ridiculous he felt talking to toys. And, more troubling, no matter how painful telling the truth might be.

Chapter 5

Truth for the Win

"¡Mami! ¡Papi!" Marco stuck his head out his door and yelled into the hallway. "¿Cuánto tiempo hasta la cena?" He needed to know how long before dinner so he could plan this out.

"Dos horas y pico," Mami answered from the first floor. Just over two hours. He had time.

"¿Necesitas ayuda?" Marco asked, offering help. "Si no, voy a bañarme."

"Gracias al cielo," she called playfully.

"Jaja," Marco laughed back. *Very funny, her thanking the heavens I'm gonna bathe.*

"¿Y el paquete?"

Marco knew she'd ask about the mysterious package. "Jugetes de baño. Solo me costaron tres dólares." He liked that he told her the truth. They *were* bath toys (sorta true; they did require a bath) that only cost him three dollars (totally true).

When she answered, "Bien," he sprinted to the basement to toss the laundry his mom had started into the dryer. He was so nervous he fumbled the dryer sheets and sent the whole box flying. After scrambling on all fours to replace them, he beelined to his parent's first-floor bathroom and snagged his mom's coconut-scented bubble bath. He wanted something more manly, but his pop didn't seem to have any. Marco had never even heard him run a bath.

Back in his room upstairs, he unplugged his radio alarm clock and carried it, along with fresh clothes and the monsters in the box, down the hall and into his own bathroom. He hadn't used his phone since shooting truck vids with Tink, and it was probably too out of juice anyway to run a countdown. *No importa.*

Once the bath water was half-way up and bubbles nearly escaped the brim, Marco stepped into the soothing warmth. The water was slippery with soap. It felt nice. He made a mental note of the time and reached over the edge of the tub to grab his monsters out of the box. He gave them a quick dunk to warm them, bent them at the waist to sit in his hand, and cleared away some bubbles so they'd be covered just to their necks. He had to slow his heart rate to start.

"Hi, um, monsters. So, um, I'm Marco." He tried to ignore the awkwardness of the one-sided conversation he was about to have. Usually when he played with toys, he gave them a voice and spoke for them. But if these toys became real, they'd have their own voices. He'd want them to. He didn't want to brand them with his own idea of how they might respond. So he just talked, like the directions said, without pretending their answers. And he spilled his guts out.

"You're probably wondering why I ordered you. It's not that I don't have friends. It's that I lost my best friend. And it's totally his fault." Marco closed his eyes and remembered talking with Maite during recess the second day of school, the day after he and Tinker fought.

"She asked me, 'What happened between you and Tink?' I didn't want to tell her because I didn't want her involved. The thing is, uh, ever since the summer tree climb, I've felt *different* about Maite, kind of impressed by her. I didn't want to say anything that might make me look... uncool... to her. Let me back up and tell you about the tree climb.

"Near the end of summer, she climbed a tree higher than any of us, to prove she could. Her brother, Knox—and I'll tell you about him later—he said she'd only beaten him because she was lighter, so she could climb higher, to the smaller branches that could take her weight. She got pretty riled about that, so she challenged him to climb the backstop behind home plate at the high school baseball field. That's a chain link fence, tall enough to stop foul balls from beaning people in the stands. Anyway, Knox said climbing that was dumb and probably illegal and he wouldn't do it. I agreed it was an iffy idea, but I also thought Knox was too scared to try. So she double-dared him. And that marked the start of my heart flipping and flopping like a fish on a pier any time I looked at her. Flip, flop, gasp."His free hand mimicked a fish breathing its last.

"Fast forward to the second day of school at recess. Maite leads me out to the kickball field, and we're waiting on the sidelines for our turn to kick. She pulls a soccer ball out of the ball bag and warms up with toe bounces. A player in the outfield yells, '¡Guarda el balón de fútbol!' Put that ball away. So what does Maite do? She does a final toe juggle, grabs the ball midair, and shouts, 'This ball's white. That one's red. There's no confusing them, so I'm not putting it away!' Monster pals, it's amazing how she stands her ground. And she's so great in a bunch of other ways. So I kinda felt like I had to tell her everything, every dumb detail.

"I tell her, 'Yesterday Tink and I were trying to decide which clubs to join. I couldn't believe the school didn't have an art club, so I thought I should start one. And that thought stuck in my head until evening when I'm sitting in a tire swing in my back yard. Then what happens? Tink comes storming across his lawn toward me. His T-shirt's soaked with sweat, and there's a smudge of grease on his forehead, and he's furious, like, practically foaming at the mouth. I'd forgotten to meet him at Old Man Jenkins's Junkyard—again.'"

Marco's chest tightened at the memory.

"Tink starts shouting, 'How could you have forgotten? Again?!' I tell him, 'Oh, man, I'm sorry, Tink.' But the truth is, I don't have an excuse, so I tell the truth. 'I just ... forgot.'

"Tink shouts and shoots his hands in the air like he's never forgotten anything in his whole life. 'I've asked you three times,' he says. 'You forgot two weeks ago. You forgot last week. And then again today after school. You keep *forgetting*.'

"And get this, Monsters, he makes air quotes with his fingers as if I didn't really forget. But I *had* forgotten, which doesn't make it better. I should have written myself a note because Tink's been waiting on me to start his new life-sized robot. But now he's yelling, 'It's a two-person job to take the hood off a 1971 International Harvester Scout.'

"'Maite,' I tell her, 'I know it's a two-person job because Tink wouldn't stop talking about it—the Scout was an early model of the entire SUV line—blah blah blah. He wants the hood, that big sheet of metal. So Tink goes, 'And that hood ain't gonna stay there forever. Someone's gonna spot that prize and swoop in and take it out from under me. I need help to screw off hinges, lift the frame, and roll it home—on *two* wagons, yours and mine.'

"I tell Maite, 'I already told him I was sorry, but by the time I get my wagon down from the garage wall where Papi hung it and we get to the junkyard, flat out running with our wagons bouncing and tipping behind us, Jenkins is in the process of chaining the front gate for the night.'

"Tinker asks him to stay open a little longer. Jenkins doesn't seem interested until Tink offers him more money for the hood *and* promises to fix his lawnmower—for *free*. The piece of junk lawnmower is a pile of parts behind Jenkins's shack. When we finally get to the Scout, Tink's so mad about having to fix Jenkins's lawnmower that all he does is snap orders at me about which screws to pull and which joints to bang out. We barely claimed the stupid thing. The next day, Jenkins tells him a collector came by asking for Scout hoods.

"The whole time, Tinker wouldn't even listen to my idea about an art club. I really felt like he only wanted me there for my work and my wagon."

Marco was quiet for a few seconds. He re-dipped his monsters under the water to warm their heads, then scrubbed some bubbles into the red monster's tentacles, like he was washing its hair. Then he realized he didn't know if the talk-for-an-hour thing allowed for breaks.

"Maite says Tink and I have been friends too long for me to think he just wants a helper.

"Monsters, Antwone 'Tinker' Tibbs and I have been friends since we were four years old. The day he moved in next door, he brought over a plastic screwdriver to help fix my toy fire engine. Only, the engine wasn't broken. But I understand now why this kid carries tools. Mechanical emergencies happen around him all the time, and he's great at tinkering. His first really big project was turning a toaster oven into a robotic dog. It would follow him and chase its tail when the toast was done. So I nicknamed the kid Tinker. It stuck.

"But Maite was soooo quick to defend him. 'He was probably just mad he had to remind you,' she says. And maybe she's right, but I don't want to hear it, so I tell her there's more. She asks, 'Wait, what happened then?'

"I told him I was going to start an art club, and I didn't want him in it. I told him he has *his* thing and I have *my* thing—and I use the same air quotes around the word *thing* that Tink used around *forget*.

And I told him we'd both be better off if we stayed doing our own things without the other because I don't like being ordered around."

Marco paused again for a moment, remembering how Maite put a hand to her mouth and said, "Oh, no, Marco. You didn't."

"Yeah, I did say that. And then Tink says he wouldn't have had to order me around if I'd been on time. And I told him he wouldn't have to worry about that anymore because we wouldn't be meeting again. Ever. And Maite says, 'Oh, Marco. You've got to take that back.' But I won't because Tink agrees with me. He says he was stupid for ever counting on me in the first place—as if I haven't gone to Jenkins's place with him a hundred times. And that place is a dump, all filthy and and smelling like gasoline and covered in grease with, like, a million rusty, jagged edges to slice yourself open. So what if I forgot to meet Tink a few times? Does he sit with me when I'm making art? Or join me in it? Never. So he has to apologize, take back his losing his cool, in the first place.

"Pero no lo hizo. He didn't apologize," Marco told his monsters, who still sat in his palms, immobile and sudsy.

"Neither did I."

Chapter 6

Soap Scum

Marco looked from his soaking little friends over to his alarm clock. He still had a half hour to go. His throat hurt. He didn't usually talk that much. But he actually had more to say if he was going to be completely honest about himself and his circumstances. And he hadn't even told them about the other Cariños. He shivered, then realized it wasn't the idea of Knox that made him do it. The water was getting cold, the bubbles fizzing to nothing.

He turned on the water to the hottest it would go and poured in more bubble bath. The water level rose to his chest. Bubbles tipped over the edge. Normally, Marco would have drained some bathwater before adding more, but the monsters' directions didn't seem to allow it. *Do tubs get heavy enough to fall through the floor?* he wondered. *Hope not.* The now-warmer water soothed his shudder. He hauled in the froth to surround his monsters in suds.

"Ever since, Knox keeps shoving and shoulder-checking me. Maybe Maite told him something or maybe that's just Knox's sour personality shining through. This week he spent all Wednesday glaring at me. Poor Rosita—that's Maite's little sister—she tries to crack us up over lunchtime reading jokes out of a book from the school library. Jokes like, 'How does a cat like its steak? Medium rawr.' and 'Why does an ice skater cross the road? To learn to do crossovers.' After each punchline, she wags her eyebrows, hoping to pull a smile from us. Maite giggles, every time, as do I. Even Tinker. But Knox scowls and tells her to stop trying to bring together people who don't belong together. It was pretty mean, to be honest.

"Rosita's library book gives me an idea, though. Fifth graders can spend lunchtime in the library if we have work to do, like writing a book essay. Mr. Farlán even lets us eat in there because he says he wants his library to be a place kids can go when they need a break. So picture it, monsters. Thursday, I spread my lunch across my lap and hide behind a wall of books, so I can avoid sitting across from Knox in the lunchroom.

"And I really did research—on you!—searching for evidence of real-life monsters. Unfortunately, most monster sightings are hoaxes, meaning they're not real. People like to paint and string cardboard cutouts between trees and snap grainy photos and post the pics online with click-baity titles like 'Sasquatch Sighting.' Qué más da.

"Anyway, I'm telling you this because the MOM Co. letter says we're supposed to be honest, and being in the library wasn't the escape I wanted. I couldn't stop looking at the Mind-imus Maximus. That's a reading corner in the library where we shared Choose Your Own Adventure books. We took turns deciding what characters would do, but, after awhile, I saw how much Tink liked making decisions, so I switched to just giving advice and I let him make the final decision on which action to take. Tink almost always got us killed before we'd finish the adventure, but it was still fun. The next day Maite comes in to the library."

Marco pictured her bursting in ahead of Rosita, who was pulling Knox, who was digging in his heels. All three stopped at his stack of books.

"So I ask Knox, before Maite can speak, what's wrong with his feet lately that he keeps bumping into me. I didn't want to outright accuse him of bullying in front of Maite because, honestly, I think she's lost patience with all of us. But ha! Monsters, it was awesome seeing the girls turn on him when he answered, 'Nothing's wrong, marciano.'

"¡Qué va! What *nerve*.

"Maite looks ready to burst into flames and says, 'Knock it off, Knox, or I'll start calling you by *your* other name.' Then Knox warns her to 'ten cuidado,' And then, monsters, Maite does the most-Maite thing ever. She snaps her fingers in his face. *So much for 'be careful.'* Rosita clasps her hands over her mouth to stop laughing. And I am *dying* to know his other name.

"The moment doesn't last though. When the girls leave, Knox stays back and gives me a warning. He says, 'Stay away from my sister. Bien lejos, ¿oíste?' *Real far, you get it?* He punctuates each word by jabbing a finger in the air. Then he leaves. And monsters, I don't know how to do that, stay away from his sister. We have classes together every day. Besides, I don't wanna stay away."

Marco looked at the clock. Fifteen minutes to go. He shivered. The hot water he added before had cooled, and he needed more. This time the hot setting wasn't so hot. It was just warm. He filled the tub to the brim. Foam sloshed over. He didn't dare add more bubble bath. He hoped his moving around wouldn't make waves roll over the top.

By now, his throat was sandpaper, but he had two more things to talk about—his folks and how he got the monster ad. Despite being on the outs with friends, he wanted the monsters to know he did have people who loved him and who he loved back. And he hoped letting them know *how* he got the ad would also show he could be brave.

"So, my folks are the best, you should know. They encourage my art and they buy me supplies all the time. They ask questions—in a good way—about what's happening in my life. We have dinner together almost every night and pretty often do game nights, which is hilarious.

"It was my pop, though, that led me to the monster ad—and you three." Marco dunked the monsters again and this time set them to float on their backs so he could scrub his feet. He was, after all, supposed to be taking a bath. The red monster's tentacles spread out and swayed like the plastic had softened.

"Just a few weeks ago, Papi decides to clear out the attic. I don't remember him ever going up there. I've never gone either. I always imagined attics filled with horrors or completamente abandonado—empty and spooky as a haunted house. But Papi drags a step stool to the second floor 'para alcanzar la puerta' and I kinda hope he won't be able to reach the door, but he manages to snag the pull ring and yank it down. There's a hinged staircase on the inside of the door, and it clunks down and nearly takes Papi's head off. And then I'm positive it'll snap while we're climbing, and we'll break our necks on that rickety thing.

"Worse, Papi warns me, 'El ático no está acabado,' and then explains that an "unfinished" attic means it isn't ready to be a living space. I think, *So it's a space for the* un-*living? Like, zombies?* But I don't say it. Papi must see my worry because he explains. 'It means da space is raw, hijo, like when da house was built. Jou will see da wood beams, like da skeleton a da house. Da walls is no finish. No hay carpeta ni lámparas.'

"*The skeleton of the house? No carpets or lamps?* I imagine wood beams exposed like ribs. Light coming from a single, exposed bulb dangling from the ceiling. I picture the bulb swinging on a cable that changes direction to try to strangle me. Or the bulb flickers out, because of course it will, and I'll see dark shapes slink into corners, *where anything might hide.*

"But, friends, I wasn't going to let my pop face the Undead alone, so I tighten my grip on my flashlight and nod to Papi that I'm ready to go up. The attic ladder is even more flimsy and unstable than I expect, especially with Papi ahead, rocking it with each step. So when I climb up to the entrance, I have to force myself through. If ever an axe is going to come down on me and split me in two, I'm sure it's then. But Papi's already through without an axe-murderer claiming his life, so I figure I'm probably safe. I finish climbing and quickly stand. The space isn't nearly as creepy as I expected."

Marco explained how light spilled in thanks to a window at the far wall and how the wooden floor was coated in dust, but there weren't any footprints, human or otherwise, dragging through it, so apparently creatures didn't live there, hiding out. Stacks of boxes pressed against the walls and leaned in where the ceiling slanted, but there was nothing so creepy as, say, a human mannequin to trigger a heart-stopping jump-scare. He had worried about finding something creepy in the boxes, though, like an old-timey porcelain doll that might come to life after its hundred years of solitude.

"It's lucky, then, that the first box that catches my eye is a type I've seen before, long and thin and made of white cardboard. I lift the lid and find a treasure trove, of old comics. I shout, '¡Guau, Papi!' *Wow.* 'Whose are these?'

"Papi pulls strings of cobwebs off is hair, and the white streaks against his black hair makes him look so much older. Totally unnerving. Anyway, he says, 'Son mios. I bought them already old. I use dem to learn Eeenglish.'" Marco imitated his father's deep baritone voice.

"'Ha! Cool way to learn a new language. Are the comics worth anything?'

"'No sé, hijo. Lo dudo.'

"'Bien.' I say, glad I don't have to wear white gloves to handle them since Papi doubts they're worth anything."

Marco remembered turning a few over in his hands. The covers were ragged, the corners bent, and the yellow pages browned at the edges. The art inside looked old school. Simple lines with solid colors, no shading. And the characters were kids, not grownup superheroes like today. Those comics were from a past generation, old even before Papi spotted them and plunked down a few coins, his price of admission into a new language and culture.

"Papi says, 'Si los quieres, son tuyos,' and with that, Papi's comics become mine."

He told his monsters how he thumbed through the comics later in his room, laughing at the ads in the back. The advertisements pitched everything from green plastic army men to teeny tiny pool tables to mail-order monsters. And he admitted that even though the thought of the Undead in his attic had scared him, he knew monsters for kids would be different. "Alive, for one thing, not dead and unsettled. And the ad said they'd be friendly. I hoped so, to me at least."

Marco smiled at his floating monsters and kept scrubbing and talking. He described his neighborhood hangouts, including the park at the end of the road and the tiny patch of woods alongside it, where he for sure knew a pair of coyotes nested their pups. He and Tink sometimes heard their yips and howls and even investigated when they thought the grown coyotes were out hunting. They found an empty den. It was a dug-out hole with a few gnawed bones left behind. He told them how he's improved at juggling a fútbol and about library trips with his folks. "And I don't know what I want to be when I grow up, but I hope it has to do with art."

Marco had never been that honest to anyone. He wondered, *Is anyone fully open with another living person? Are parents this honest to each other?*

He had no idea.

After exposing his soul like that, he needed a moment to relax his voice and his senses. He checked the clock. The hour had passed. The green monster's yellow fringes were saturated brown, and the patterned monster had gone all white, like its color had bled. Marco didn't know if those things were bad, but he decided to trust the directions and keep going.

He scrubbed extra hard to remove all remnants of the day's filth—but carefully too so water wouldn't slosh over the edge more than it already had. He was only mildly surprised to find dried paint behind his ears. The bath water got good and grimy—and freezing—so Marco plucked up his monsters and turned the silver handle to drain it. He dried himself with a fresh towel, and his monsters with his T-shirt which was plenty stinky after his sprint home.

The water gurgled as it spiraled down the drain. Sure enough, there was an impressive grey ring of soap scum around the top third of the tub. Marco ignored it. He used his towel to sop the water and bubbles that had spilled onto the floor so it wouldn't seep through and leak downstairs. Then he gently placed his monsters in his shirt back into the tub. He dumped the rest of his clothes around them to form a nest and wished them a happy transformation.

Is that a thing, a happy transformation? He decided that, yes, it was. The bath had been transformative, whether the monsters changed or not. It had lifted his spirits and washed away his troubles, if only for a little while. He had so many emotions about Tinker and his other friends that he had needed a boost—no matter how or what would come of it.

Chapter 7
Faith

"Mami, Papi," Marco said as he entered the dining room, the smell of coconuts wafting behind him. His parents took a deep, exaggerated breath, putting their hands to their hearts.

"Jaja," Marco laughed, glad he smelled better than when he arrived after school. He had another mess in his room to clean: the box, its filler paper, his wet towel, the contents of his backpack that he'd spilled everywhere, but at least he returned his alarm clock to its spot. He pulled out a chair for his mom and sat as his pop set out the last of the food.

"If you go to my bathroom, would you please leave my toys in the tub?" Marco asked. "I'm, uh," he struggled to find a reason, but after opening his soul to his monsters, he was in a truth-telling mood. "I'm seeing if they expand in water. I'll clean the tub tomorrow. Promise."

His pop nodded as he sat, "Bien, mijo. I had water-grow toys too, when I was little. Dey were sea creatures. Mis juguetes crecieron desde pequeño hasta el tamaño de mi mano entero."

His toys grew from being tiny to the size of his full hand? Marco hoped his own possibly-coming-to-life, new-best-friends would get much bigger—enough to change his life forever. He figured they'd probably grow to, like, seven or eight feet tall.

"Ten cuidado con esos," Mami said. "No te tragues ninguna parte de ellos."

Marco forced himself to not roll his eyes. *Of course I won't swallow any part of the toys. Do you think I'm a baby?* But his mom's expression was serious, her eyes penetrating and so black that he thought staring into them was like swimming into the deepest expanses of space. And then he understood. A kid who swallowed part of an expanding toy would have something big and bloating in their belly or intestines. That'd be really bad. He nodded.

Better change the subject. "Gracias de nuevo, Papi, por darme tus cómics este verano. Ordené los juguetes, los monstruos, a través de un anuncio en la parte de atrás." As long as he was truth-telling, he came clean. He thanked his pop again for giving him his comics and told him, easily, breezily, that he'd ordered monsters from an ad in the back.

His pop crooked his eyebrow. "Imagínate, esas empresas todavia en negocio." Yeah, Marco was equally surprised that the company was still in business. Maybe it was the only one.

With a clean conscience, Marco could enjoy one of his favorite meals, piñon vegetariano y arroz con gandules. Puerto Rican plantain veggie lasagne with a side of rice and pigeon peas. The combo never tasted better.

• • • • ● • ● • • •

Just before bedtime, Marco checked in on his monsters to see if there'd been any change. *Huh.* They weren't bigger or moving or anything like that. *But did I leave them lying like that? All tipped over and messy?* He pushed the tentacles off the face of the big one, unbent another's arm, and brought the clothes around them a little closer to better prop them. Then he trudged back to his room and tapped a finger onto his finished truck, testing for tackiness. He had added a coat of clear varnish the night before to brighten the colors and make it shine. Satisfied it was dry, he set the truck in a box and put the box in his closet. *That was a fun project.*

Marco tumbled into bed feeling accomplished and more relaxed than he had in a long, long time.

He was well fed and had poured his worries into the bathtub. If the monsters were the same in the morning as they were straight out of the box, he'd definitely feel duped, but there wasn't really anything more he could do that night except the very last bit.

And that might be the hardest part.

The directions said to have faith.

Marco closed his eyes and admitted to himself that the past few weeks had been awful. Being alone, without friends, made him feel like driftwood rocking in a vast and violent sea. He didn't like this school year. He wanted it to be like his other school years, when he could laugh effortlessly and joke around with everyone. He wanted his new monsters to come to life. To be his friends. To see what life might be like with them. He wanted them to grow and be real.

Please be real.

He drifted off to sleep wondering what the next day would bring.

Chapter 8

They're Alive!

Marco bolted upright. His room was dark except for weak light peeking around his window curtains and the bright blue numbers on his clock, which read 6:30 a.m. *Sunrise. Estupendo.* His folks would still be asleep.

He threw off his blankets and shivered at the chill. Normally he'd stay curled up a bit longer, enjoying the silence, maybe picturing his next art project. But at that moment, all Marco wanted was to get to the bathroom and welcome his new, giant friends.

He couldn't believe how much, all night, his mind had been chewing on the idea of monsters. He dreamt of them, huge and impressive, their mere existance enough to jar anyone. They'd be so amazing that Tinker couldn't help but realize how cool

Marco was and what a big mistake he'd made in pushing him away.

Marco set his feet on the carpet and padded down the hall to the bathroom. He turned the doorknob. The *click* wasn't loud enough to wake his folks but, oddly, it didn't cause a stir inside the bathroom either. *Shouldn't something be moving around in there?* Nervous, he slipped inside and tiptoed toward the bathtub. Nothing jumped out at him. If the monsters were big and hulking, wouldn't he see them by now? Or had they escaped?

The closer Marco got to the bathtub, the more he suspected something was wrong. When he reached the bathtub's edge, he peered in. He expected to see his clothes in a jumbled mess in the bathtub, the monsters long gone because they'd escaped to the underside of beds, the scariest parts of any house, where all monsters awaited their victims to end their days and suck on their bones. Or, he expected to find his monsters scrunched up in the tub, still in the midst of their giant transformation. Or, he expected they'd drop from the ceiling, where they'd held themselves for hours waiting to jump-scare Marco to death.

But what he found wasn't any of that.

His monsters were still wrapped in his dirty clothes. They were bigger than when he'd gotten them, yes, but they'd only plumped up to about a foot tall, about the height of a cat. Yes, they'd grown more than his pop's water-grow toys. But this—*this?*—is all they were?

How can this help me?

Marco swallowed the growing lump in his throat and put his hands on the edge of the tub to lean in. The monsters looked different, besides being bigger. He stared until he figured out that their skin wasn't rubbery or plasticky anymore. *Had the hot water melted their coating? Or had it made the fluff or whatever was inside them split their shell so they popped up like popcorn? Maybe their stuffing was folded neatly inside their plastic casing, like a parachute in a pack, waiting to be deployed, but instead of a kid having to pull a cord, they just had to add water.*

Marco leaned in further until he was face to face with the stinky green one. It smelled exactly like what he'd expect a toy to smell like after it had been soaking in dirty, wet clothes. *Uf! Powerful!* It looked so lifelike.

Why would MOM Co. feed kids lies about monsters being friends and then make the monsters look so lifelike if all this was just to make foot-tall, water-bloated action figures?

Marco was about to pick the thing up when he thought he saw its mouth move. A twitch. He stared hard. Nothing. Not a flutter.

I'm losing it.

He leaned in even closer.

The monster's eyes popped opened.

"Whoa!" Marco jolted upright at the same time the monster lurched forward, and then, with a "*KAH-AHHH,*" the creature coughed up the cuff of a sock.

Marco scrambled backward, and the monster did the same, slipping on sopping clothes and soap scum. When Marco stopped moving, the monster did too except to lift its green hand to its mouth and pull out the sock, grimy and grey and dripping with goo.

"Ew," said Marco and the monster, together.

Marco froze. "Did—did you just speak?"

The monster nodded.

Marco re-approached. They leaned toward each other, angling for a closer look, until their noses nearly touched. "Cool," they said in unison, amazed with each other.

Marco jolted again. He held out his palms, willing time to stop. "Whoa. You talked."

The other two monsters moved beneath the bundles of clothes. They clambered out and shook themselves, like wet dogs, before meeting Marco's eyes.

The red, furry one still looked like the biggest of the bunch, but it was a foot and a half tall, tops.

Marco suspected the tentacles on the top of its head and the fluff of its fur made it look bigger. Those tentacles waved left and right as if still underwater, swept in an invisible current.

The final monster, the one with different patterns across its skin, now matched the grungy clothes. It would have disappeared entirely if Marco hadn't seen it *change* to match.

"Whoa," Marco said. "You—you can camouflage."

"Camouflage," it repeated, mimicking his voice.

He shook his head. Marco could not believe these *things*, these former toys, were understanding him. And answering too. But they were. He realized his...disbelief... was making him act...strange. He didn't want to be rude, even if he had just thought they were *things*, so he said, slowly, "Cool. Should we call you Camo?

"Camo," it said, while tilting its head and nodding, like it was introducing itself.

A low growl near the water spigot made Marco turn his head warily. The noise came from the big, red monster, the one that looked most wild and threatening. *Would it attack?* Marco wondered. He spoke softly to it, just in case. "And what do you do, Friend?"

The monster stopped growling to shake its foot free from Marco's pants leg. It closed the gap between itself and Camo, then, with a nod signaling some kind of unspoken approval, hoisted Camo overhead like a baser lifting a cheerleader.

"Ooooh," Marco said. "You're strong. And your growl is fierce. How about we call you Growler?"

Growler lowered Camo, quivered the tentacles on its head like a feathered crown, and tapped a fist to its chest. Marco took all that to mean yes.

He then turned back to the green monster who'd coughed up the sock and raised an eyebrow in question. The monster stared back until the air surrounding it shimmied like heat waves in the sun and turned a bit smoky-looking. A smell like his mom's coconut bubble bath wafted off it and filled the room.

"Ha! Cool skill." Marco leaned over to open the bathroom window and let out the coconut fog, then returned to the bathtub. "Can you do other smells?

The air shimmied once more, and the bathroom filled with the smell of rotting fish.

"¡Fo! Stinky!" Marco waved a hand in front of his face. "Stop, please!" He grabbed his bath towel off the hook and flapped it toward the bathroom window, driving the stench outside. "We'll be lucky to not wake my folks."

"Stinky sorry," it said

"Your name's Stinky?" Marco asked before realizing he himself has said the name first. The monster simply adopted it. "Ha! Awesome! Nice to meet you, Stinky!"

Camo took a step toward Marco and said, "Should we call you Marco?" in a perfect imitation of both his question and his voice.

Marco's face split into a smile. *Wow.* "Um, yes, please," he answered. "Call me Marco. I—um—wow, you all talk. That's so amazing. And excellent. I'm so glad."

He watched them step around the remaining clothes, heading toward the wall of the tub, and asked himself what he had expected. *Did I think they weren't going to talk or understand words even though MOM Co.'s directions said to talk to them?* Still, their talking was a pretty spectacular thing, something he was hugely happy about.

Growler pushed Camo up to reach the bathtub edge. Marco leaned in to help them all out. As he did, he thought again about their size. They weren't huge. But maybe he had been wrong to want that. Maybe their size was all right. *How could I feed huge monsters, if they need feeding? How could I hide huge monsters? And I'd for sure want to. If the world saw real monsters, they'd be captured and taken away, right? And most important, how could I take them to school and show them off? So, small monsters are good. Better even. They can hide in plain sight, always be around— unlike certain ex-friends.*

He set his new monster pals and dirty clothes on the bathmat. Then he swept the clean towel across the inside of the tub to wipe away the lingering, crusty soap scum. He felt good about keeping his promise to clean up. Plus, now he could start the day chore-free before his folks even woke up.

He couldn't wait to see what these living, mail-order monsters could do.

Chapter 9

Friendships Can Be Monstrous

Marco dumped his dirty clothes and the totally-alive monsters onto his bed. Their eyes lit in delight at the mattress's springiness, and in silent agreement, they started bouncing.

"Wheeee"—(bounce)—"this is fun."—(bounce)—"Later"—(bounce)—"let's play ball!"—(bounce). At top height, Stinky flipped backward like a footballer nailing an overhead kick.

"Let's challenge"—(bounce)—"the coyotes"—(bounce)—"to a grrrrrowl"—(bounce)—"contest." Growler bared his teeth, but Marco thought it more likely the coyotes would make a snack out of him.

"Awhoooooooo!" Camo's head tilted back to perfectly imitate a howling coyote.

"Whoa," Marco said, lowering his palms for quiet. "Guys, let's go outside."

"Whoa," Camo said, imitating Marco's voice. "I'm a girl."

"Oh." Marco looked at all three monsters, who were slowing their bouncing. He couldn't see any difference between them except their obvious colors and styles. "And you two?"

"Boy," they said in unison.

"Okay then." He quickly decided not to call them *guys* anymore as a collective. "Cool. Let's go outside. Lemme figure out transportation."

Marco left them rolling on his bed while he disappeared into his closet looking for his biggest backpack. By the time he pulled it out, all three monsters were wrestling.

Camo had Stinky locked in a Half Nelson. *Where did she learn that move?* Even more impressive, every time Growler dived to try to tackle them, Camo made herself invisible and yanked Stinky out of the path. Growler twice landed where they'd been and slipped on something gooey. Marco leaned in to investigate and was shocked to see Stinky releasing light blue slime every time Camo rolled him.

Guau! Great defense mechanism. He's making himself harder to grab. Marco ran his finger through the goo and raised it to his nose. *Mmmm, smells like gummy worms.*

Growler hoisted Marco's pillow, ready to drop it on his challengers.

"Okay, colegas!" Marco called. "Let's go."

Growler, beneath the upheld pillow, and Stinky, successfully free of Camo's grip (*Is there anything slime can't do?*), tilted their heads. Camo was nowhere to be seen. *Where is she?*

"Colegas means buddies or pals."

Camo appeared solid white at the top of the headboard, her arms raised like she'd been ready to leap off it and bodyslam the pillow to crush her brethren underneath. *Cooool.* Marco deeply regretted stopping the action.

"So, um. I'll carry you outside in this backpack, so no one sees you walking. It'll be a tight fit." Marco reassessed them. Growler was taller and bulky, but the other two were skinny. That would help. "And, hey, it'll be best if grownups don't see you moving on your own and talking and, well, acting alive."

His monsters tilted their heads in question.

"Um, grownups aren't used to seeing living monsters, and they might, I don't know." He looked to his closet wishing he didn't have to tell them the harsh truth of this world. "They might get scared or try to capture you like you're animals or something or," he looked back at them, "maybe even take you away."

They straightened. Camo flashed red. Growler growled. Marco didn't want to give Stinky a chance to respond in his own uniquely stinky way.

"It's just a better idea not to draw a grownup's attention. Kids are no problem. Kids know there's magic in the world." Marco thought about the biker guy at the post office who assured him magic exists. "And some grownups know magic is real too, but better to be safe than sorry. Whenever you see grownups, go limp like a toy. If they've seen you move, don't worry. I'll confuse them. It's easy. I do it a lot. I just start talking fast, especially in Spanglish. It intimidates a lot of 'em. Strange, I know. Anyway, we'll have a lot more fun playing this way."

That last sentence must have done the trick because his monsters smiled and climbed into the backpack. Marco tore off his dragon-print pajamas and grabbed grey cargo shorts, grey ankle socks, grey-but-once-white sneakers, and a yellow T-shirt with a green fútbol and the word "GOOOOOOL" screaming across it. He hefted his bulging backpack onto his shoulders before tiptoeing downstairs. He scribbled a note for his folks that he was going to the park at the end of the street and schlepped his cramped monsters past the playground to reach Coyote Woods, as he called them. *No one will see us here*. He sat and tipped back for his monsters to crawl out.

Camo raised her face and arms to the sky and twirled like a ballerina in a music box. "Blue!" she shouted and turned the exact shade. *Fascinating.*

Growler curled his hands like ice-cream scoops and dug in the soil. What he was looking for, Marco didn't know, but he didn't care how dirty they got. *That's what baths are for.*

Stinky was the last to do anything. He stood immobile for half a minute before conjuring a thin fog with the sharp, pungent smell of fall. Marco closed his eyes to experience it better, absorb it. He filled his lungs with the melancholy, unmistakable scent of the changing season. Marco could smell still-warm breezes and sun-baked mud. He got woozy on the sweet tang of turning leaves and the rot of fallen fruit. He caught a whiff of withering plants hunkering down for the upcoming winter, as if saying goodbye, promising to return in spring.

With his eyes still closed, Marco heard bees buzzing and was both grateful he'd slowed down enough to hear them and sad that he wouldn't hear them much longer. They'd need to bed down for the cold too. He learned last year that bees hibernate. This year, he learned the word "susurration." It means a soft murmur, like a whisper. When Mrs. Kroppert asked the class to put the word in a sentence, Marco said susurration was the sound leaves make when wind rushed through them. That earned him a rare smile. It was the easiest smile he'd ever earned. Wind cascading through trees was his favorite sound in the whole wide world.

When Marco opened his eyes, his monsters were gone. He whipped around, scanning the woods for any sign of them. *Noooo! I've lost my monsters on my first day—my first hour, even!*

"Colegas!" he shouted, cupping his hands beside his mouth. He wanted to yell *Come back!* or *Don't leave!* but something stopped him. *I-I can't ask that of them,* he decided. *They're living things con suficiente coco to make their own decisions. Like Camo going blue, doing what she wants, she's got say-so. Tiene autoridad.* Marco opted instead for, "Where are you?"

A growl answered him.

Either that's Growler or I'm about to become coyote food. Do coyotes eat people? Surely coyotes wouldn't be allowed to exist in his neighborhood if they hunted people. But maybe they'd attack if they felt threatened. Marco froze. He wasn't that close to their den, and it was daylight, and coyotes hardly ever prowled by day. *Still, this is their woods, not mine.* Then another question hit: would his monsters abandon him at the first hint of danger?

The growl intensified. Marco finally registered that it was coming from his feet. He looked down and spotted not a coyote baring its teeth but Growler, covered in black earth, standing in a giant pit. The hole he'd excavated was nearly as deep and wide as Marco was tall, and he could've dropped right in. *Prolly a world record how fast Growler dug that.*

Marco spotted another pair of eyes blinking up from within, followed by a smile directly underneath. The teeth were smeared with dirt. Stinky. Just as happy as could be.

"Is Camo in there too?"

A seemingly empty spot in the pit flashed neon red like a beacon before disappearing once more.

"You are so cool," Marco said, wondering if Camo still stood there or had already moved. "And you two too. Growler, let's hear how loud you can get."

Stinky clamored to get out of the pit and left another panicked trail of light blue slime. But he didn't make it before Growler drew in a breath, lowered his tentacles—making them look more like dreads than ever—and let loose a bellow loud as a blast of dynamite. It would've bulldozed a lion. Marco slapped his hands over his ears.

"Whoa! That's awesome!" Marco shouted as Stinky clamped onto his leg, clumps of black soil crumbling off his quivering frame. He peeled Stinky off and patted his head.

"Don't worry, Stinky. If there were coyotes nearby, that seismic roar sent 'em running, fer sure. Now, let's fill in this hole and go deeper into the woods." He pointed at the tallest tree, a giant, soaring oak with branches low to the ground and uppers sporting great fall color. Those high branches were too thin to hold a human, but his monsters would be able to go topside, and he knew their view through those leaves would be an amazing vista into a daring new world.

He and his monsters tossed soil into the hole, all four scooping through their legs like dogs, their butts hanging over the pit's edge. When they were done, Marco felt, more than saw, his monsters tag along behind him. They climbed every tree they could. They dug holes. They played tag. They collected branches to make stick forts. Eventually, Marco surrendered to hunger and exhaustion. By the sun's place in the sky, he knew it was early afternoon.

"Monstruos," he called from the lowest branch of a crabapple tree with a fiery red canopy. "I've gotta go back home to eat."

"We eated already," Stinky answered. It sounded like he was one tree over.

Marco's brows furrowed. "What did you eat?"

"Leaves," he answered.

"Flowers," said Camo. She was nowhere to be seen.

"Bugs," answered Growler, standing up from within a pile of leaves and pushing a beetle flat-handed into his mouth.

Gross. "Ugh, okay, well, I eat people food, and my folks will expect me to show up for it. Let's go play inside for awhile."

He heard rustling and spotted movement, and Stinky and Camo soon joined him, covered in dirt and twigs and leaves. They shook themselves before climbing into his backpack for the walk home. Marco had to leave his shoes outside the door with a shouted promise into the house to clean them later. After settling in his room and changing into clean clothes, Marco went downstairs for a late lunch. He asked for extra food for his monsters.

"¿Tus jugetes tienen hambre?"

"Sí, Mami. My monsters are really, really hungry." He was glad to be telling the truth. "Tres más bocadillos, por favor."

His mom laughed and made him three more sandwiches besides his own. "Que comes todito," she admonished with a wave of her finger.

"Don't worry, Mami. We'll eat all of it."

His monsters gobbled the sandwiches and barely stopped at the plate.

That's gonna be a problem, Marco thought. But he considered that if they ran out of human food, his monsters could always sneak outside for beetles, plants, or whatever else they wanted to eat. He told them it'd be okay if they did, but it'd be better to do at night and after a few days to get to know the neighborhood and for sure with some warning so he wouldn't worry about them.

For the time being, though, Marco wanted to keep his monsters hidden, keep them a surprise until Monday when he could bring them to school. He wanted to reveal them to his shocked classmates and show them off as the greatest friends a person could have. There was still daylight left. Marco didn't want his monsters to get bored in his room, so he came up with an easy, brilliant, scary idea.

"Homies, let's go play in the attic."

Chapter 10
Leveling Up

Camo squealed and set off her best display yet: thick stripes, the colors of the rainbow, scrolled down her body like she was a digital billboard repeating on a loop. If that wasn't what happiness looked like, Marco didn't know what was.

"Attic be stinky?" Stinky asked.

Marco had to think about that. "If dust has a smell, yeah."

Growler dropped to a crouch and flattened his tentacles along his back to come to a point, like an aerodynamic helmet. He growled low.

"What's wrong, buddy?" Marco asked.

"You said the attic was scaaaaaarrrry.."

"Oh." Marco ran a hand though his hair, unwittingly making it spikier, remembering his bathtub talk. "Well, I was scared going in, but it just turned out to be dirty, not dangerous. And we'll be together, right?"

Growler's growling got quieter until his tentacles relaxed and drooped, some curling into question marks like cats' tails,. He straightened to stand.

"So it's settled. Everyone grab a toy."

Stinky snagged sand toys. Camo unplugged the radio alarm clock and strapped it to her back with its cord, like a jetpack. Growler pushed his hands into huge, green-foam boxing gloves.

"Smash," Marco said, to Growler's delight.

Marco chose building blocks and his big bag of marbles and set them beside the door. "Okay, colegas, wait here a sec." He ran down to the kitchen pantry and hooked over his shoulder the same step stool his pop used to reach the attic door.

"Oye, ¿qué haces?"

Marco startled. His mom rounded the corner. Her voice carried suspicion.

"Voy al ático, a jugar." He *was* going to the attic to play but kinda felt his mom's raised eyebrow was justified. He'd only been there once before. *Maybe it does seem odd.* "¿Puedo?" He waited while she considered whether it was allowed. When she nodded, he went on his way.

Lugging the step stool up the stairs was a beast. *These stupid things are made for the tallest, strongest people,* he thought with a grunt, *and they're the least likely to need them.* When he finally reached the landing, he set the stool under the the high door and returned to his room.

"Bueno, vengan." He grabbed his toys and waved his monsters toward him. "Let's go."

Growler knuckle-walked in the toy fists like a gorilla, straight out the door. Camo camoed into the alarm clock she was carrying, looking like one clock carrying another out. *Very techy.* Stinky set the sand bucket on his head and promptly walked into Marco's leg.

"Here, let me take that. I might need your help." Sure enough, when Marco reached the top of the step stool, he wasn't tall enough, even on his toes, to reach the pull ring. He looked down to his monsters. "Feel like climbing?"

Growler leapt. Marco gasped. It was scary having a monster spring at you, even if the monster was only a foot tall. Growler's stuffed fists couldn't grip Marco's shirt but his back nails easily did. Marco held back yelps as Growler clawed his way up to stand on Marco's shoulders.

"Come, Stinky," Growler ordered, and Stinky crawled up Marco like a lizard, much less stabby than Growler but much more stinky. *Whoo, I gotta request a nicer smell as his default.* Once Stinky was presumably on Growler's shoulders—Marco couldn't risk looking up to check—Camo started up, a radio with legs. After some jostling and weaving that made Marco nervous, he heard Camo call down, "We're still too short."

Before Marco could think what to do, Growler shifted, and Camo shouted in surprise. Their column swayed and teetered. "Steady!" he called.

"Got it!"

Marco heard the terrifying sliding of stairs and leapt off the step stool, taking Growler and Stinky with him. They rolled onto the landing just as the attic stairs pounded the carpet, six inches from their heads. *Way too close. But it worked.* Camo dangled from the door's pull ring.

"Nice job." Marco stood.

Camo flashed pink and swung onto the extended stairs. Everyone followed her up.

"Whee, duuusty!" Stinky sang as Growler and Marco stepped into the attic and Camo plugged in the radio.

"I knew you'd like it." Marco laughed as he strode over to the window and heaved it open. "How you doin, Growler?" When he didn't hear an answer, he turned and saw his biggest, most fearsome monster shaking. He ran to kneel beside him. "Whoa, what's wrong, buddy?"

Growler didn't answer. His hackles rose. His eyes widened. He stood immobile.

Marco followed his gaze into a corner where an old-fashioned, wooden rocking horse tarried, waiting to be called back into action. It was his old horse, from when he was a toddler. "Growler, buddy, that's not alive."

Growler pointed at it with his boxing glove. "S-s-snakes."

Marco squinted toward the relic. Just a normal, old-timey horse. He stared until...*Oh.* "Growls, those aren't snakes. That's rope. The horse's hair is made of rope."

Growler's eyes were round as golf balls, so Marco marched over and grabbed a handful of mane. "See?" He batted it around a bit. Pulled some. "I'm not hurt. It's just rope, not snakes."

Stinky and Camo walked over to stand beside Growler, whose red fur still bristled.

Marco frowned. He yanked off his shirt and draped it over the horse's mane. Then he turned the horse around to face the corner. The horse didn't have a tail, so there was no more visible rope. Growler's hackles settled. Marco sat cross-legged beside him. "Está bien, hombre. It's fine. We know you're fierce. That's why you're Growler. And that's why you'll smash."

Growler looked at Marco, walked to the back of the horse, and punched its butt with his giant green fist. He growled a super growl. Marco followed it with shouts of his own.

• • • ● ● • ● ● • • •

By the end of the day, Marco had no idea how he hadn't gotten into trouble.

Once Growler got over his initial horse misgivings, he spent a half hour growling and roaring, maybe trying to convince himself he was worthy of his name. Marco shouted in between Growler's growls so his folks might believe it was him making the racket. When his voice got hoarse, he asked Camo to imitate him. She was thrilled to, as she'd already mastered imitating guitar riffs and drum solos from the radio.

She's epic, Marco thought.

When Growler stopped roaring, he tested how many stacked boxes he could carry at once. Two high, five high, eight high overhead. Stinky bulldozed his shovel across the dusty floor. *Shhhhhhhh* one way, *Shhhhhhhh* the other, pushing powder across the floor like he was plowing snow. When he piled enough grime against the wall, he scooped some into his sand bucket and tipped it into his mouth.

"¡Uy! Stop that!" Marco scrambled over from the center of floor, where he'd been stacking his building blocks. "That's bad for you!" He snatched the shovel from Stinky, accidentally flipping half the filth onto his white socks.

"Why bad?" Stinky asked, big-eyed and innocent. Marco sighed. In truth, he didn't really know *what* might be bad for monsters, although he suspected eating dust older than him might not be a good thing. Marco felt bad for snatching away Stinky's toy.

"Why don't you just have fun scooping the dirt? I'll toss it out the window so our place here is clean, and I'll get you a snack later."

"Okay."

Marco picked up the bucket and had just chucked its contents out the window, like a farmer pitching a hay bale, when a gust of wind blew it all back to his face. *Poof.* It billowed around him like a confetti bomb—a very grey confetti bomb. Before Marco could clear his eyes, Stinky scrambled up his leg and licked the grit off his face.

"¡Uy!" Marco repeated, raising a hand to block him.

"Yummy dirt." Stinky leapt into the bucket in search of dregs.

"Seriously, don't. A*h-kah!*" Marco's cough expelled a cloud of dust.

"Ooh." Stinky must've found a particularly tasty bit of feculence because he released a stink-cloud of hot garbage.

"¡Fo!" Marco fanned his hands at the window. "That's it. I'm getting y'all some food." He dropped through the attic entrance, skipping the rickety staircase entirely, to the second level of the house, then bound down the stairs to the kitchen, where he snagged some bananas. By the time he climbed back to the attic, Stinky was twirling his sand spade through cobwebs like he was spinning spinning cotton candy. Before Stinky could eat it, though, Marco threw him a banana. He tossed another to Growler, who barely caught them without dropping a box.

Uh oh, where's Camo? Marco spotted his marbles, the ones Tío Juan had given him, outside the velvet bag. He knew he hadn't opened the bag, and he knew he had 20 marbles. But it looked like there were double that number there. And they were piled up weird.

"I see you, Camo," Marco sang and tossed a banana her way. Half the marbles stood, and Camo snatched the snack mid-air. Food gave Marco a little break from shouting and monster-sitting, and they all played until dinner, when Marco's pop told him he was glad Marco had a new place to play, especially since he was cleaning it up.

Uh, I am?

He considered this. His folks must've thought the scraping sound was sweeping. He nodded to his pop. *I guess I'll clean if I wanna cover our tracks.*

That night, his first with monsters, he slept with them under his bed. They didn't want to join him when he patted his pillow or even when he made blanket nests at his feet. It was the closet or under the bed for them, they said. So he pushed some blankets and pillows under his bed and threw a big sheet over the top to drape over the side. It made a fort over a monster's natural habitat, the space under a kid's bed, where they could pop out later to eat him.

Marco hoped he'd survive the night.

Chapter 11

Maite

Sunday, he woke up—surprise, he was alive!—to an unusually cold day for mid-September. The cold offered an excuse to stay in, though that's not why he did. He wanted secrecy. A knock on his bedroom door, though, right after breakfast, changed everything.

"Maite está aquí y quiere verte," his mom called through the door. As if that was a normal thing. A not-earth-shifting thing. As if, "Maite's here and wants to see you" wouldn't flip his heart up, down, and sideways. *But of course Mami wouldn't know that.*

"¿Aquí donde?" he called back. It was important to know where "here" was.

"Al otro lado de la puerta," came the answer, not from his mom but from Maite.

¡Jolín! On the other side of the door?! "Dame un segundo," Marco called back, desperately needing a few seconds. He was in his pajamas—his too-small pajamas that ended mid-shin and featured robots and space aliens and UFOs in a galactic war with laser beams crisscrossing his chest, which was now thumping with the horrifying possibility of Maite seeing him wearing PJs he begged his folks for two years ago when he was on a big sci-fi kick. But his PJs weren't his biggest problem. His monsters were sprawled across his bed reading comics, the very ones their ad had come from. "Colegas, red alert! This is not a drill! Hide, hide, hide!"

They scrambled off the bed and climbed bookshelves and pulled drawers and leapt into his closet. They made a racket, knocking over books and soccer participation trophies and boxes of space shuttles and action figures. It all thudded or clanked or crashed. The monsters clumsily hid behind things way too small to cover them, and they couldn't have made more noise doing it.

"No, not there, Growler! Move! Camo, what are you doing? Just camouflage! Go invisible! That's your whole *thing*! Stinky, pull that blanket over you!"

"Marco, ¿qué está pasando?" Mami asked, rapping at the door again.

"I'm putting some stuff away, Mami. And I've gotta change. One second."

His mom asked something else he didn't hear because he was pulling his pajama top over his head. Growler chose that exact second to start growling, and Marco had no idea why except to guess that maybe his flight-or-fight instinct was kicking in.

"Cool it, Growler," Marco said as he stripped off his matching PJ bottoms which screamed "Pow!," "Blamo!," "Ka-thunk!," and "Crash!" in yellow and red and blue, only to find a worse horror. Zombie underwear. ¡*Maldita sea!* "One more sec!" he called to his mom.

Marco grabbed the nearest clothes, jeans that weren't what he would've preferred to wear in front of Maite and a blue-and-white striped polo shirt that gave a dressed-up vibe. He kicked some clutter under his bed and launched toward the door, tripping on a syrup-coated plate that just a little while ago held a huge stack of pancakes he'd brought up for the monsters. He yanked open the door before his mom or Maite could get suspicious. *Or more suspicious. Whatever.*

"Hi! Hi, Mom. Maite, hi." He tried to hide rubbing his toe into the carpet to soak up syrup. He hoped no one noticed. "Hey, come on in."

His mom gave him that questioning look moms sometimes do, that microscopic squint that doesn't thin their eyes at all, hardly changes their expression, yet tells anyone who really knows them that they are *so* suspicious. It was a full-on what-are-you-up-to glare.

"Wanted to clean up a little, Mami," Marco said, tilting his head. It sometimes worked.

"Ah, está bien," she answered and moved aside to let him see Maite behind her.

"Come on in, Maite." Marco had said it a million times. The Cariño and Torres families were friends before Marco was born, so he'd grown up with Knox and Maite and Rosita, and it was totally normal for them to hang out. At least it would seem that way to Mami. To Marco, though, there wasn't anything normal anymore about seeing her.

She sidestepped his mom and sat down on the foot of his bed, the one place not covered by comic books. "Gracias, Señora Torres," Maite said, thanking her. His mom turned, and Marco heard her steps retreat down the stairs.

"Hi." Her full attention, that one word, kinda belted him across the face.

"Hi." His voice cracked, and he hoped, as he cleared his throat, that she didn't notice.

"I'm not really here to play," she said.

You're here to express your undying love, Marco thought, suddenly realizing his feelings were so extra. *We've known each other forever and I can't tell her I have feelings that I don't have for other friends. And if she liked me back, what would that even mean? Would we hold hands? Last year I'd've thought that was gross. Now? Not so much.*

He realized he hadn't answered and was maybe staring at her. He spun toward to his boombox, an attic find, and pressed Play to start the CD in the slot. He wanted noise to cover their conversation, though he didn't believe his mom would purposely listen. Still, she might accidentally hear something. The music was slow, the singer whispering about soft hair. Marco fumbled for the Next button. Better. Something peppy. He raised a brow at her, what's up?

"I want you to make up with Tinker. Let's walk over to his house and negotiate a truce."

So this is about Tink and me, not her and me. It's about peacemaking. Marco felt a teeny tiny stab in his heart. She was only thinking about friendship. *You know, the sort of relationship you've always had with her,* he chided himself, *because she's not thinking of anything else.* He wouldn't be able to share his feelings just then. If ever. *Maybe I'll take that topic to the grave. Which is better, really, because what do I want? To be her boyfriend? And, like, take her places?* Marco frowned. *Stupid feelings.*

Maite must've taken his frown as a *no*. "You can't stay angry at him forever, Mar—" Her eyes darted to a spot over his left shoulder. Marco froze. That's where Camo was hiding.

"What were you saying?" Marco asked, stepping to his left to block her view.

"What is that?" Maite asked, pointing. Her attention was laser focused, cutting past him to the bookshelf. "Something moved. Did you get a hamster?"

"Yes," Marco blurted. "I got a hamster, and she's loose, but don't worry, she likes my bookshelf, so she'll leave you alone, and what were you saying, you want me to go with you—"

Maite's eyes went wide as his pancake plate. Marco's heart skipped a beat. *Think fast.* "Hey, let's go to the kitchen. I'm starving." *I'm not. I just had breakfast.*

"What on earth?" Maite jumped onto his bed just as Camo landed at Marco's feet. Maite scrambled backward until her calves hit his headboard and her back slammed against the wall. Camo appeared just like she had in the ad, with different animal patterns across her body.

Marco pressed the heel of his hand to his forehead. *Whyyyyy is she showing herself?*

Camo pointed at Maite and said, in a perfect imitation of Marco's voice, "Ever since the summer tree-climbing incident, I've felt different about Maite, kind of impressed by her."

Marco gasped and stumbled forward to try to press a hand over her mouth, but Camo put both hands over her heart and replayed his confession, "Flip, flop, gasp."

Too late. Marco covered her mouth anyway and then pressed his own lips together. He shut his eyes in humiliation and thought back to when he'd spilled his guts to his monsters in the bathtub. He hadn't told them not to tell others. It wasn't Camo's fault. *And Maite must have figured this out, right? That I'm crushing on her? Knox sure knows it.*

Marco opened his eyes, which were still trained on Camo, and sort of, kind of, a little bit wanted to catch Maite's eyes and see her reaction, see if she understood exactly what Camo was saying, to know whether he should ever show his face to her again, or if maybe she didn't totally hate what Camo was implying. But before he could peer up at her, as if fate was trying to ruin everything about him, a pile of boxes in his closet collapsed and spilled their contents across the room. Stinky rolled out with them. Realizing his cover was blown, Stinky crouched and whipped up a smell of chocolate and whipped topping, maybe as good a smell as any to win a girl's heart.

"W-what are THOSE?!" Maite shouted.

There's no hiding this anymore. Marco had wanted to keep them secret, and he totally could have, he reasoned, if the perfect girl of his silly dreams hadn't crashed his mess of a room to ask him to do the right thing, at least in her eyes, and turn him into mush.

"They're-they're monsters," Marco admitted. "And there's one more."

Growler burst out of the nightstand, sending the wooden drawer crashing. He growled forcefully enough to create an impression. Maite jumped off the bed and pressed her back to the wall farthest from him. But she didn't leave the room, even though she could've. *Huh.*

"¡Marco, por favor, baja el ruido!" his mother called from somewhere in the house.

"Sí, Mami," he answered, glad she'd only asked him to turn down the noise rather than her coming up to investigate. He turned to Maite. "They're monsters, and, before you ask, yes, they're friendly, way better friends than Tinker or Knox."

Maite's attention whipped from Growler to him.

Oops, didn't mean to mention Knox.

"Wait," she said. "They're monsters? Like, real monsters? And they're f-friendly?"

Whew. She thinking about the monsters more than Knox or my flopping heart. "Yeah, they're friendly to me and my friends. That includes you." Marco immediately understood why Camo revealed herself. *Maite's a known friend, and Camo's curious..*

"Amazing," Maite said, a little breathless. "Monsters. How do you have monsters? Wh-where did they come from? Why are they here?"

"Maite, I-I really don't want to say. You'll find out soon, but not today, okay?"

Maite looked him in the eye for a long while. It was unnerving. Finally, she nodded.

"Until then, meet Camo," Marco swept his hand above Camo's head as if presenting a prize on a game show. Camo turned herself light orange with stripes like a tabby cat. "This sweet smelling fellow is Stinky." Marco bent to pat him on the head, and Stinky rose and took a bow. "And that big guy is Growler. He's intimidating but will be as friendly to you as you are to him." Growler nodded at Maite as if unsure whether to surrender to her charms.

"Hello," Maite squeaked. "Wow, you're incredible, all three of you."

Camo stepped up to Maite and raised her arms like a kitten asking for upsies.

Maite's jaw dropped. "Is she—are you—wanting me to pick you up?"

"Looks like it," Marco answered. Camo mimicked him.

Maite scooped her up as if she'd always cradled monsters, but Camo soon climbed to Maite's shoulders, straightened, and swan-dived onto the bed.

"Great form," Maite said with a laugh and plopped down beside her. She reached under the bed to extricate a cardboard box overflowing with plastic zoo animals.

She remembers where those are? They hadn't seen use in a long time, especially, Marco thought with chagrin, since he hadn't played with anyone lately. Maite set a panda on the bed. Camo immediately morphed to match it, and Stinky joined in with a zoo smell.

"¡Uf, Stinky, please," Marco begged. "Something nice?"

Stinky's expression changed, and soon the room smelled of fresh hay. Growler tore paper into strips, and Maite galumphed an elephant toward it to dip its trunk in. "Mmm, delicious." Marco bounced a tiger over to feed in total harmony with the surrounding herbivores. For a blissful hour, they played "zoo" and other games the monsters initiated and read comics until Mami called up asking if Maite wanted to stay for lunch.

"No, gracias!" To Marco she added, "I'm helping Mom make arepas for dinner." She stood. Marco's chest felt a bit emptier at the thought of her leaving.

She turned toward Camo with open arms. Camo accepted the invitation—*who wouldn't?*—and hugged her fiercely, turning a glittery silver. Growler stepped up next for his hug. *Huh, that's surprising, showing that much affection, but, again, it's Maite.* Finally, Stinky held her.

"I'm taking them to school tomorrow," Marco said. "I want them to be a surprise."

"Why would you take them—oh. It'll be a surprise all right." She looked away and paused so long, he didn't know if she'd forgotten what she was going to say. But she went on. "I'm not sure that's a good idea. Are they going to be okay?"

"I'll take care of them."

She crinkled her eyebrows. Marco didn't know what that meant, but her attention was devastating, so he decided to keep his mouth shut. "Marco, I'll keep their secret. But promise to think about fixing things with Tink, okay? And, about Knox, I don't know what's going on, but I can tell you two things. First, Knox is protective of Rosita and me because he's big on family loyalty. Second, he doesn't like being teased about his size. It's not always great being bigger than others. If Knox is mad at you, Marco, there's probably a reason. Maybe ask yourself why."

She hugged him goodbye. He was glad to have bathed the night before.

By bedtime, Marco was in the tub again, his new pals cannon-balling into the deep end. It'd be worth the cleanup.

"Well, that was fun, playing with Maite, wasn't it?"

"I'm not really here to play," Camo said, bubbles atop her head, perfectly copying Maite's voice. "I came over to ask you and Tink to make up."

Marco felt himself deflate. "Yeah, well, she doesn't understand." *I have to show Tink and Knox that I can have great friends without them. Jealousy can do a lot to balance the scales.* He thought about the next day, when all his classmates would see his new friends for the first time. *They'll fall over in shock.* He smiled to himself. *Monsters. Mis colegas. My spectacular pals.*

I can't wait to see everyone's reaction.

Chapter 12

The Reveal

"Muévanse," Marco urged his monsters. "We gotta go!"

He had hoped to get to school early, but Growler was taking forever, combing and re-combing his red fur and slicking back his tentacles with Papi's hair pomade and mumbling about his first day of school *ever*.

"Will that glop slime up the inside of my backpack?" Marco asked, raising an eyebrow.

"Stinky'll be in there," Growler replied.

Marco got the point. What's a little slime when you'll *definitely* have stench? He sighed, then yawned. *Wish I coulda slept better.* He spent an hour after lights-out explaining what school was and how classes went and what the schedule was like and the school layout. Then, after he convinced the monsters to try out the bed, he realized what a bad idea that was. The mattress kept dipping and rising from the monsters' play. They even walked across his chest. *Total disregard.* He had left out fruit and granola bars—bars being the clear favorite—and considered finding them other nosh like nightcrawlers or moths in case they got overnight munchies. *Who knows what they'll want to eat before a new adventure? Maybe they'll stress eat.* But he couldn't leave the window fully open for them to find their own food and maybe get lost.

He did open the window a crack, though, because Stinky spent the night experimenting with different scents to make his best first impression on the schoolyard.

"Everyone love onion rings," he said sometime just before sunup, apparently decided.

Mostly true, Marco thought, himself not loving the idea of his bag smelling like onions.

Camo was the only monster who didn't do anything special to prepare.

"I'll be hidden," she explained. "Reconnaissance." Stinky tilted his head at her and she clarified, "Snooping."

"At least show yourself when I intro you, okay? I'd like everyone to see all three of you."

She nodded and, right there, camouflaged to look just like the mirror behind her.

"You really are very cool," he told her.

"You really are very cool," she repeated in perfect imitation.

"Thanks." He laughed and shrugged into his favorite black hoodie. "I know it."

He had to admit, though, that he absolutely couldn't look cool running to school with his heavy, monster-laden backpack bouncing from neck to butt and chafing both. *But that's the cost of subterfuge*, he thought to himself as he turned the corner to school. The usual big crowd was waiting on the sidewalk for the doors to open in just five minutes.

"Hey Fart Knox," Marco said when he reached his group. It was the first time he'd ever called him by the secret name he and Tinker used behind his back. Tink's eyes went wide.

Knox turned and balled his fists. "What did you say?"

"¡Ha!" Rosita barked and slapped her hands on her knees. "Fart Knox. That's even funnier than his real name-"

"Quiet." Knox barked. He stepped toward Rosita to tower over her.

"Don't even *think* of intimidating her," Maite said, shoving her twin bother's shoulder and barely moving him. Knox was bigger than his twin in everything but attitude.

"Yeah, Knox," Rosita said with a lilt in her voice. She raised to her tiptoes and leaned her head in. "Or should I call you—"

"Rosita, stop," Knox warned, his tone even sharper than his body language.

"You know," Maite said to him, equally threatening. "I don't like you being pushy." She stood like a ram ready to lock horns. "And this alias, 'Knox,' it's not you. You know who you really are, and you shouldn't dishonor the family by shaming your real name."

"Maiiiite," Knox threatened, "don't say another word."

She narrowed her eyes in challenge. Rosita put her hands on her hips and mimicked her sister's face almost exactly. Same slitted eyes. Same jutted lower lip. Marco stifled a laugh. *She really is doing a great job teaching her little sister to stand up for herself.*

When Rosita was sure the stalemate was over, she asked Marco, casually, "Whadya wanna say before?" as if the whole family squabble hadn't just interrupted Marco's first brave moment in a long time. It wasn't easy for him to call her brother "Fart Knox" to his face.

"I want you to meet some new friends," he said and set his backpack to the ground.

Maite turned sharply. "Although there's also nothing wrong with your old friends."

Well, a few of us are all messed up, Marco thought. From Tinker wronging him, to Maite wanting them to still be friends despite the wrong, to Knox's bullying, to the obliviousness of everyone at the school who didn't take Marco's side or didn't care about this *very important* fight. The only innocent human friend he had, as far as he was concerned, was Rosita.

"Nothing's *wrong* with us, Maite, but—"

"But what?" she asked.

But some of us don't have a brother and a sister at home to keep us company, and some of us haven't lost our best friend. Marco knew those thoughts were true and made fine answers, but neither was her fault. Nor was it her fault that he spent *weeks* feeling lonely. True as all that was, those answers felt a little too close to his heart. He didn't want to get all blubbery, especially now. "Having a few more friends is always good, right? And wait'l you see these."

Marco dropped to a knee and zipped open his backpack. Before he could pull apart the flaps, fur and tentacles rushed out. Marco backed up and straightened to stand just as his monsters scrambled up his torso to his head and shoulders.

Their deafening *"ROOOOOAAAAR!"* left his ears ringing.

The scene became pure pandemonium. More piercing even than the ringing in his ears were screams higher pitched than dolphin whistles and shouts of "Whoa!" and "What the-" and "¡Jolín!" His classmates' reactions were exactly what he'd hoped for, and their chaos rippled in all directions. Kids backed away or tried to get closer or stood frozen, wide-eyed, jostled from all sides or falling over each other. Marco had created bedlam. And it was so, so satisfying. *Chévere*, Marco thought, knowing at least some kids would think the monsters were cool. But anyone watching from down the street or, worse, through the school's windows might think Marco had set loose a rabid dog. *And that's honestly way more likely than monsters*, he thought.

Yet there they were, Stinky on Marco's head and Growler and Camo on his shoulders. Growler jutted his arms forward like a hockey player and fluffed his fur to be even more imposing. Camo pulsed shades of red. No one could mistake it for anything other than a warning.

Marco sought out Tinker for his reaction. His ex-bestie and the Cariños had been tossed about in the commotion, but Marco spotted them. Tinker's mouth hung open yet he managed to keep his eyes trained on the monsters. Marco knew he was dying to ask how Marco made monsters? He, the tinkerer, would never think of magic—but what else could they be?

He next looked to Knox, whose eyes showed—*wow*—fear? He had never seen Knox's eyes tremble. Those eyes flicked to Marco's, and Marco took the moment to lean in, hoping Knox would get the message: *Leave me alone already.*

He immediately sensed Maite's stare. She was the only one in the whole schoolyard not jostling or screaming or whispering or pointing at the monsters, but he didn't think that was out of courtesy. *If Knox is big on family, maybe Maite is too, and she probably wouldn't like him scaring her brother, even it was self-defense.* He nodded her way—*meaning what?* he asked himself—but didn't try to convey more. Instead, he found Rosita, who was smiling, face bright, as if monsters were the most natural thing in the world. She especially took a shine to Camo. She blew kisses and waved her over. *Whoa, can Rosita tell Camo's a girl?*

Marco felt his monsters push off his head and shoulders and saw them land on the ground. Half the crowd stumbled back from them and half surged forward. A few reached out to touch them, but the monsters defended themselves with a swipe of their paws.

"Whoa!" Marco yelled. "Don't touch."

The kids backed up just enough to avoid swiping range. An instant later, Marco was bombarded with questions from everyone but Tinker, who was angling for a better view.

Then phones came out.

Uh oh. Marco realized too late he'd forgotten about phones. *What was I thinking?* But phones weren't top of mind for him. He hadn't used his own since making truck vids with Tink. And phones weren't allowed in class, so he didn't take his to school. He knew Mrs. Kroppert would absolutely delight in confiscating his if he dared bring one to class. *And no way would I leave my phone in my jacket in the coat hall. Duh.* But plenty of kids did bring theirs to school, and they had them out now. A dozen pointed his way, one already livestreaming Growler.

There was nothing he could do to stop it. The last thing he wanted was to have video floating in the ethos of him slapping phones out of hands, like a criminal. *And fer reals, people don't believe anything on the internet, no matter how many videos they see or how many angles.*

"What are *those*?" Tinker demanded. Marco returned to the chess match at hand.

"These are my friends," Marco replied in the non-answer of the century.

"No. What *are* they?"

Someone in the crowd answered, "They're pets with weird haircuts to look like mini-monsters. I've seen videos where people make their poodles look like pandas."

"No, those *are* monsters!" said someone else.

"No, they're tech toys," said another voice. "Like, super advanced service dogs. Obvs."

Camo stomped her foot, drawing attention, and camouflaged to meld into the sidewalk beneath her. That sent a few kids falling over themselves for distance and a few stepping forward to sweep their hands across the space she'd been. But they touched nothing. *She must've moved.*

"Marco, what's going on?" Clarita's voice surprised Marco. She was class line leader and self-appointed top cop. *Rule-abiding Clari. Thinks-she's-in-charge-because-she's-Kroppert's-pet Clari.* She didn't talk to him much since he wasn't top of the class, and she practiced what Mami called "transactional relationships," a tendency to make friends based on what you can get out of them.

The school bell rang. A teacher flung open the doors and called, "Happy Monday! You all seem very excited to start a new week. Everyone inside, please."

"Marco, what's going on?!" Clarita repeated as everyone on the sidewalk processed that they were expected to enter the building.

"Quick, in!" Marco told his monsters before anyone else could grab for them. His monsters scrambled into his backpack. He threw it over his shoulder and sprinted inside, leaving everyone, including Tinker and the rest of his friends, out on the sidewalk, stunned.

Chapter 13

On Everyone's Lips

"MARCO! WHAT'S GOING ON?!" The voice pursued him as he sprinted toward Mrs. Kroppert's room. He'd get in trouble if a teacher saw him run the halls, but he was doing a lot of that lately. His footfalls echoed ahead of Clari's, who kept calling. Marco slammed into the doorframe of Mrs. Kroppert's classroom, the second time in two weeks, and skidded onto his seat. He opened his backpack, lifted the top of his desk, and unceremoniously dumped his monsters inside. They fell in a heap and tumbled over his pencils, rulers, and glue sticks.

"Ow!" Camo complained. "I don't fit." She crawled over Growler and Stinky and glommed onto Marco's hoodie, sliding into his kangaroo pocket and curling up so her feet didn't stick out.

Marco was glad she moved quickly, but he looked like he was carrying a rolled-up towel. "Sorry, colegas. I didn't even think about you maybe not fitting. Anyway. Calladitos for now. You gotta stay quiet 'til recess."

Saying that out loud revealed another flaw in his plan. Lying in bed that night, inhaling Stinky's weird experimental smells, Marco decided he couldn't let his monsters interrupt class or they'd be captured and sent to the secret government lab growing more real and ominous in his imagination every day. And he knew he couldn't leave them in his backpack in the coat hall because someone would try to find them, maybe even take them. Or, they'd get hungry and wander out. So what option did he have other than to keep them in his desk? Thankfully, he had a plan, sort of, to preoccupy them for a while.

"Have a snack, homies." He tossed a granola bar into his desk before lowering the lid. He wedged pencils at the edges so the lid wouldn't close and leave Growler and Stinky in darkness. They'd have air, some light, and a 270-degree sliver-view of the classroom. Camo would have more. *Maybe that'll be enough to keep them occupied, although they're mighty cramped*. Marco slid the seven remaining granola bars, all chocolate chip, from his bag to his kangaroo pocket, just in case. *Camo won't eat 'em all.* They made his already bulging pocket oddly lumpy.

Mrs. Kroppert entered the doorway just as Clarita slammed into her and then bounced off. Clari apologized, then hissed at Marco on the way to her desk, closest to the door, "What. Is. Going. On?" But Marco ignored her. He took the opportunity as she settled into her seat to hustle to the coat hall and hang his backpack on his hook. He scurried back to his desk just as the rest of the class spilled in, again prompting Mrs. Kroppert to demand that everyone slow down.

"My goodness, you all are so excited to start the day. But I suppose that's good because today we're covering sentence diagramming, and that takes stamina."

"It takes cold-blooded cruelty," Marco heard someone say, but they were in a crowd, so neither he nor Mrs. Kroppert could tell who said it. Some kids laughed. Others were still raving about monsters and pets and scientifically advanced toys and sci-fi holograms and mind tricks. They were arguing over what they'd seen and heard, and some were already gaslighting others, trying to convince them, for some reason, that they hadn't seen what they thought they had, that they were mistaken. The power trips of mind games made Marco's stomach turn.

His classmates kept talking loudly even as they worked their way to their desks or wound past him to the coat hall entrance, everyone staring him down along the way.

"Where are they?" Clari asked, stopping at his desk.

Give people a little power and see what happens? This, acting like she's owed answers.

"Where's his hook?" someone asked from the coat hall, as if the hooks weren't labeled.

Marco crossed his arms and leaned his elbows onto his desk. In an instant, Mrs. Kroppert stood over him.

"What do you have, Mr. Torres? I'm hearing your name on everyone's lips."

"Nothing," Marco answered and tapped the underside of his desk with his knee. He hoped the move would get his monsters' attention if they weren't already listening.

"Open your desk, Mr. Torres."

A few classmates rushed in from the coat hall and crowded her.

"To your seats, everyone. This does not involve you."

Marco generally didn't like it when teachers were bossy, but in this case it bought him time and would prevent anyone from laying hands on his monsters. He again tapped the underside of his desk with his knee before lifting the lid just enough for the pencils to slide in and not draw attention to the fact that he was purposely keeping the lid propped. After he felt the pencils settle, he fully opened the desk's top. Two monsters lay limp inside.

Mrs. Kroppert reached in and lifted Stinky.

Oh no. Of all the monsters to inspect, she chooses Stinky?

She turned him over in her hands. The monster looked, for all the world, like a plushie, only a bit floppy, slightly under-stuffed. Instantly, the space around him smelled like onion rings, a totally plausible scent for a toy pulled from a kid's backpack. Mrs. Kroppert replaced Stinky in Marco's desk and turned over Growler where he lay.

What is she looking for? A hidden compartment to hide candy? What?

"Why did you bring these stuffed animals to school, Marco?" Mrs. Kroppert asked.

"Um," Marco hemmed. "I had an ... *off* kind of night." It was true, he reasoned. Last night and this morning were way off the norm.

"Those are his new *frieeeeeeeends*," Knox taunted.

Mrs. Kroppert slowly turned her face his way. "We all deal with things in different ways, Mr. Cariño." It was the most enlightened thing Marco had ever heard her say.

He remembered the first week of school, when he got fed up enough to complain to her that Knox was calling him marciano. "He won't quit," Marco told her. Her too-easy response was to the class at large, "Now, kids, no name-calling," and kept on teaching. When Marco complained a second time—that same day—she pointed out that "Knox's last name, Cariño, means affection in Spanish, so maybe if you show Knox some affection, everyone could get along." *What does she want me to do?!* Marco remembered thinking. *Hug the bully?*

"While stuffed animals aren't banned at school," Mrs. Kroppert said, returning her attention his way, "I won't accept you playing with them during my lesson or allowing them to distract others. Keep them in your desk, Mr. Torres, or they will end up in mine." With that, she turned to make her way to the front of the class.

"See, toldya it was a trick. They're not real," Clari told the boy behind her.

Marco snatched a pencil and paper from his desk so he wouldn't have to open it again and quickly repositioned a few extra pencils to prop its lid.

He glanced at Maite, seated nearly opposite him in the front, right-most desk, and saw her raise a finger to point at him. She mouthed, slowly, jabbing her finger with each word, "That. Won't. Work." He didn't want to believe her, so he shrugged, then looked at Tinker. His ex-bestie was staring back with one eyebrow raised.

Marco looked to the front of the class and focused hard to keep from smiling. This was exactly what he had hoped for when he ordered mail-order monsters. He wanted to shock and amaze his friends. He wanted them to see that he was fun and interesting and that they shouldn't take advantage of him and expected to work at Old Man Jenkins's Junkyard and always do what Tinker says without Tink returning the favor. He wanted Tink to see he could survive without him. And he wanted Knox to recognize that Marco wasn't totally defenseless and alone.

The grin he'd been trying to hold back spread across his face. Despite what he'd told Mrs. Kroppert, he wasn't having an off *day*. In fact, this felt like one of his best days ever.

Chapter 14

Escape

Half an hour later, kids still glanced over their shoulder at him, missing pointers on sentence diagramming. Mrs. Kroppert grew increasingly frustrated, turning from the smart board more than usual, calling student's names and tapping the board with the blunt end of the stylus.

Marco didn't give her any reason to blame him. He faced forward, took notes, and even raised his hand to answer her question about whether the word "slowly" was an adverb or an adjective. "Slowly is an adverb, Mrs. Kroppert." He said it so properly and politely that if he was someone else looking at himself, he'd call himself a teacher's pet. But his courtesy worked. He seemed blameless while everyone else was obsessed with plushies that weren't even on display.

"Eyes up front!" Mrs. Kroppert demanded. "If one more person turns to look at Marco, everyone will lose recess today." Her eyes settled on Knox—even though his last name *does* mean affection. Marco normally hated when authority figures punished large groups for the actions of a few, but she had asked for their attention multiple times already. Each time she did, Marco felt his desk shake a bit.

Shake

"We bored," he heard Stinky whisper.

"Draw," Marco whispered back.

A short while later...*Rattle*

Marco looked down to see the word "hungry" written in crayon on scrap paper held up to the crack by Growler. He slid them a granola bar.

A short while later...*Wobble*

"Camo out," Stinky complained. He wasn't wrong to sense an injustice.

Camo stretched out in Marco's pocket, letting her feet dangle, before climbing half-way up his front. She did it slowly, camouflaging so well that he doubted anyone noticed.

"Eyes up front," Camo whispered, imitating Mrs. Kroppert, as if his teacher's admonition made Marco feel any better about her moving around. *Is she nuts? Even if she's not seen, what about the other two? Won't they be mad about being trapped?*

Sure enough. At each shake of the desk, Marco had to whisper suggestions on how to keep themselves busy and then slide them another bar. But there'd been seven shakes. Marco was out of bars. And he was pretty sure Tinker saw him slide in the last one.

He looked up in time to see Mrs. Kroppert turn toward her desk. She made eye contact, apparently checking that he wasn't causing distraction. Marco tilted his head and blinked innocently. Mrs. Kroppert wasn't swayed, but at least she stopped watching him. She reached her desk and tugged on a drawer. Just as she did, Marco's whole desk skidded left.

Screeeeeeeech. His desk's tiny, metal footplates scraped horribly against the floor tiles. He realized, to his horror, that his monsters were revolting against their imprisonment. His desk ended up a foot out of alignment, rocked there by monsters in cahoots. Keeping his body still, Marco shifted his eyes to see Camo pointing left, leading her brethren in rocking the desk. Marco then looked up to see that, yep, their movement had drawn the attention of half the class, but *only* half. The other half was watching Mrs. Kroppert tug on her drawer.

"Apologies for the noise," she called. "This drawer sticks, and it can take the whole desk with it." She settled on a knee and ducked her head, apparently to inspect the trick drawer. "It won't budge." She tugged again. *Screeeeeeech.* Marco's desk moved the other way.

The class nearly rioted.

"Mrs. Kroppert! Mrs. Kroppert!" Clarita cried out.

"Your monsters are doing that!" Roberto shouted.

"¡Colegas, no!" Marco whispered, sticking his fingers into the desk to reach one.

Mrs. Kroppert looked up from under her desk, the blue shadows of her cheeks bluer than ever, her eyes wide in alarm. "Class, get ahold of yourselves!" she demanded. "You're all so agitated today. My desk is heavy and makes noise when it's moved." As if to prove it, she yanked the drawer again. It flew open. She fell to the floor, and her desk did indeed move—a few inches and made a teeny, tiny squeak. All eyes turned her way as she scrambled to her feet.

"This is what comes of allowing toys in the classroom," she said, half to herself and half to her students. "Imaginations run wild." Marco thought that was pretty unfair, expecting kids to stifle their imaginations, especially when it comes to toys. But his monsters weren't toys, of course, and every kid in that class knew it.

Mrs. Kroppert bent down again to rummage in her desk just as Marco's desk bounced up and down like his tío's low-rider. That hooptie's hydraulics made the front of the car jump six feet off the ground. Marco's desk went only six inches off the floor, but that was plenty.

"Found it!" Mrs. Kroppert called and held up a cloth cube bigger than her hand. It had words on each of its sides, but Marco couldn't spare any attention to read them. His desk shook. He flattened himself across its top. Mrs. Kroppert raised an eyebrow his way.

"Still feeling off, Mrs. Kroppert," he said. "Just wanted to stretch a bit." The truth was, he had a feeling his monsters were gonna pop.

"A game might help you feel better." She walked toward the smart board and rolled the cube across the floor like a die. It drew all eyes, so Marco felt safe enough to sit back.

That's when the monsters made a break for it.

He watched, aghast, as his desk top popped open and pencils, paper, and crayons flew in every direction. It looked like he'd set off a string of firecrackers in his desk. And what were the firecrackers celebrating? His monsters' breakout, of course. The desktop slammed down with a crash. In that nanosecond of noise and confusion, Growler and Stinky leapt out of his desk, high into the air—Camo directing them, Marco presumed, as he couldn't see her—and, clearing his head, thudded onto the desk behind him. That was Santiago's seat, and that kid was nervous enough without having monsters land on his desk. "Chillaba como un cerdito perseguido por un gallo," as his mom would say. He squealed like a piglet chased by a rooster. *Yeeee, yeeeeeee.*

Desks screeched as kids pushed away or scrambled out of their seats altogether. Marco spun in his chair to track his monsters and try to snag them. In that moment, he saw two classrooms: the one behind his desk, and the front of the class visible in the windows' reflections. These were the windows that last week showed his hair looking like a porcupine. Marco almost *wished* for such a simple humiliation—because *this*, this moment, was waaaay bigger trouble.

Movement in the reflection caught his attention. Mrs. Kroppert was prat falling, tripping backward. The noise of his exploding desk must've startled her. Maybe she bent to pick up the cube and overshot standing up.

"¡Santos, son vivos!"

"They're really alive!"

"Dey escaping!"

"They're gonna eat us!"

Kids shouted from all directions.

Marco barely caught sight of Stinky, who was piggy-backing on Growler, grasping his tentacles like reins. It was too perfect to not have been planned. *Schemers.*

Growler, with vaquero Stinky, launched off Santiago's desk and clambered onto the cork board between windows. He scaled it as easily as a cat climbing a tree.

Beside them, T-style pushpins seem to move by themselves, staggering a few inches at a time, fast as lightning. Marco spotted Camo, camouflaged brown like the cork board, her outline just visible with each hoist.

Marco caught Mrs. Kroppert's reflection awkwardly stand just as Clarita vaulted to her feet and shrieked, "MARCO! WHAT'S GOING ON?!?!?!"

He couldn't have answered if he'd wanted because, just then, Growler and Stinky scrambled into the air vent above the cork board. Growler's hand reappeared through the slats for a fraction of a second. Camo flashed pink, presumably in happiness, and clasped his hand for a final heave into wild freedom. Growler roared in triumph.

Girls screamed.

Boys shouted.

Everyone pointed.

Marco felt a cold wave of dread crash over him.

Apart from the classroom clamor, other classes might have heard that roar echoing through the air ducts, the sound bouncing through the sheet metal ductwork snaking around the school. More importantly, Mrs. Kroppert would have certainly heard something, what to her would be an inexplicable sound.

He had no choice.

"Brrrehhhh!" He pretended to retch.

Kids already on their feet recoiled.

Those few still in their seats pushed their desks away again. More squeals of metal on linoleum.

"Brrrehhhhh!" This time, Marco covered his mouth like he was holding something back.

"What's happening? What's all this noise?!" Mrs. Kroppert bellowed from the front.

"I think I'm gonna throw up!" Marco cried, adding a convincing whimper at the end. "I need to go to the nurse!"

"Go, go, go, go!" Mrs. Kroppert shooed with flapping hands, dusting him away.

Marco was struck with a brilliant thought and lifted his desk lid, pretended to scoop something out, and bent over while running out of the room so that *just in case* the kids told Mrs. Kroppert about the monsters escaping, she could check his desk, see that they're gone, and reason that he'd taken them to the nurse's office for comfort.

But now he had a much bigger worry than a teacher thinking he was barfing all the way to the nurse's office.

His monsters were loose in the school.

And there was no way they wouldn't wreak havoc.

Chapter 15

Squeegee Needed in Aisle Four

Marco speed-walked through the halls with no intention whatsoever of going to the nurse's office. He could hear scratches overhead as his monsters scuttled through air ducts. Marco tried to follow the rectangular, metal air shafts, but he couldn't walk through walls or into classrooms while they scurried above both. Making things worse was that sometimes the ducts hung below the white, foamy ceiling tiles, and in other places the ducts were hidden above them. Throughout, they connected at joints. His monsters would have access to the entire school.

I'm gonna lose 'em, he worried. He tried picking up the pace what little he could, but outright running would draw attention. He ran a hand through his bangs. The halls had security cameras. Even without them, it was *annoyingly easy* for teachers to keep track of kids. Half the grades had only one teacher, so kids were glued to their class. Grades four and up had two or three teachers, but their rooms were right next to each other or across the hall, so their worlds weren't much bigger. And all the grades shared the Specials rooms for PhysEd, Art, Tech, and Music. Between all those adult eyes, there was almost no way to avoid detection.

Marco rounded a corner and skidded to a halt. Halfway down the corridor, the principal was talking with the janitor. *Disaster.* Marco flung himself back around the corner and pressed his back to the wall. He held his position about two seconds while juggling his options.

Option A: stay there and hope they didn't come his way.

Option B: run like mad in the opposite direction and hope he'd make it to the next hallway, parallel theirs, to keep up his monster chase. Option B would for sure have him running past open doors with all their prying eyes and maybe even colliding with someone else prowling the halls. But he was *ahem* supposed to be sick, and he could claim delirium and fright.

Option B was it. He ran for it.

The hallway stretched before him, seemingly without end, reminding him of when he stood on the shores of Lake Michigan and tried to spot land on the other side. He heard it was possible on a clear day, but nope. He'd never seen anything but waves and sky. The lake was endless. The hallway was endless. And he thought he heard voices coming nearer.

When he finally reached the corner, he ducked around it, again slamming his back against the wall. All he could hear was his heavy breathing and pounding heartbeat. He turned his head, listening for clues of where to go. No more human voices. No overhead scuttling.

¡Caracoles! Marco thought. *I've lost 'em.* The gravity of his situation lashed him like a freezing gale. It stung. It tightened his lungs. Made it hard to breathe. *I got monsters*—Marco's heart pounded faster. *Brought them to school*—his lungs weren't working. *And now they're loose in the pipes*—the air was soup. *They could leave the school and I wouldn't see them. They could go into the city and I couldn't stop them. They'll terrify people or get hurt or lost.* He tried to think what to do next but his brain was fumbling and stumbling. He felt woozy.

A high-pitched scream tore through the silence of the halls and shattered his panic.

"Camo!"

Was that Rosita?

Marco gulped whatever air his body would allow and raced toward the 4th-grade wing. As he passed open doorways, he noticed kids inside looking out or at each other, no doubt wondering where the shouting started. When he got to where he thought Rosita might be, he crept to the door to peek in. Only his forehead and one eye was visible to anyone looking out.

Rosita's teacher had a hand on the shoulder of a girl wearing a red campesina top under a jean overall-dress. "What was it, Lola? What did you see?"

Rosita sat directly behind her and noticed Marco's eye. She flashed her eyes wide, meaningfully, before looking up at the air duct vent right above the other girl's desk.

"I saw eyes. Up there," the girl, Lola, replied.

"Oh, don't worry, dear. It's not a person. It's too small for people. There's probably just an animal caught in the air system."

Rosita scratched her chin sideways with a finger, pointing further down the hall.

Marco retracted his head from the doorway in case her teacher looked his way. He had no idea where any air ducts led in this building or any other. But if Rosita was pointing farther away from where he'd come, that was the way to go. He only got past three classrooms before he heard pounding footsteps behind him. He dived into a bathroom and peeked out.

It was the janitor hightailing it into Rosita's room. *The teacher must've called for 'im.*

Marco knew he was running out of time. Chances were, the janitor would catch him or his monsters. Marco darted out of the bathroom and ran pell-mell down the hall. When he reached the next corner and turned left on a guess, he was elated to hear more noises from above. He skidded to a halt. The scratches and scritches and scrapings and jostling moved toward the right, across the hallway. Then there was a pop, a thud, and a clatter.

It echoed, resoundingly.

"¡Colegas!" Marco wrenched open the door to his right, a door he'd never noticed before. Inside were Growler, scrambling out of a bucket, Stinky, who'd fallen onto a wet mop, and Camo, who he could only see because she was covered in dripping yellow paint.

The janitor's closet, Marco realized. It was stocked with brooms, a big garbage bin on wheels, shelves of individually wrapped toilet paper rolls, and a gallon-size can of paint covered loosely enough to allow Camo's fall to tip the top and slide her right in.

"Oh my gosh, are you alright?" Marco asked instinctively.

Stinky smiled, ecstatic. Marco again heard running footfalls.

"Hide!" Marco shoved Growler into a mound of red feather dusters and hoped his fur would blend in. He set Stinky on a heap of dirty green rags and told him to "make like cloth." He didn't have to move Camo at all since she was standing in front of a yellow "wet floor" sign.

He hurled himself back into the hallway and through the next door—open, thankfully—just as the approaching footfalls rounded the corner.

Marco's eyes had to adjust. A single nightlight cast a dim glow over a grey, paint-splattered utility sink and rows of spray bottles and cleaning supplies lining grimy metal shelves. The stench of chemicals stung his nose and dizzied his logic. A dozen mops leaned into the far corner. A tiny, two-inch-tall wall surrounding a drain on the floor kept mop water from spilling everywhere. Marco stared at the tiny embankment to remind himself not to trip on it on his way out, after the janitor got what he needed in the other room and moved on.

What would the janitor be looking for? Marco wondered. *An animal trap? Poison?*

He was hoping the janitor would be quick and leave, oblivious to the fact that he'd been in a room with three monsters. Marco heard the door next to his open, then some jostling, then a clang, and finally a man-scream nearly as high pitched as Lola's, the girl in Rosita's 4th-grade class. The door next to his own banged open against the hall wall and swung back on its hinges while, apparently, half the room's contents spilled out and smashed across the floor. Oh, and his monsters were roaring. And laughing. Both, actually.

There was nothing else for it. Marco slammed open his own door, hoping to scoop up his monsters and escape. *To where? Maybe the nearest mountain to live out my days avoiding capture?* Instead, he was thrilled to see the janitor had the yellow paint bucket on his head, its contents sliding down his face and body and splatting onto the smooth tile floor. His limbs windmilled as he slipped and slid to the far wall, all while screaming, "Monsters!" at the top of his lungs. The bucket's thin metal handle was caught under his lip. He looked like a soldier wearing a too-small helmet. But it wouldn't take him long to regain his balance, pull the handle free, and wipe the paint from his eyes.

Marco plowed ahead with his plan. He hooked his monsters in the crook of his elbow and, instead of escaping to the wild sierras, sprinted down the hall, around the corner, and into a bathroom. He dumped his monsters into the long sink with six taps and turned on three.

"You've got ten seconds!" he barked. Even that seemed too long. The commotion down the hall grew with the obvious addition of other grownups. After counting to ten and watching his monsters turn from yellow to their normal colors, he hauled them into his arms and hotfooted it to the main office. He had just slipped into the nurse's station when Mrs. Kroppert walked in.

"Oh, you're here," she said.

"Yes, ma'am." Marco answered. His shirt was soaked with sweat and water that had dribbled off his monsters. He watched her eyes flick their way. They were slouched on the cot beside him, propped against each other as any lifeless plushies might be.

"Well, there's been some excitement in the school since you left the room."

Marco raised his eyebrows in mock curiosity.

"Animals in the air ducts. Squirrels, probably, but big enough to frighten the janitor into thinking they were...something else."

"I haven't seen any squirrels," Marco reported helpfully.

"Mmm, yes, well, does anyone know you're here?"

"I don't know, Mrs. Kroppert. I just came in and sat down." It was true. He did come in and sit down. He just didn't emphasize how he'd *just seconds ago* sat down.

By the time Mrs. Kroppert found the harried nurse—who'd been sent first to check on Lola and then the janitor—Marco was ready to call it a day. The nurse felt his still sweaty forehead and damp shirt and decided to send him home. As he waited on the school's front stoop for his mom, his monsters laughing and jostling in his backpack, he knew he had to come up with a better plan for tomorrow. He nearly melted with relief when he heard the school secretary in the main office scold someone on the phone, "Well, it's not right we have to wait three whole weeks to get our security system fixed. Yes, I know we're not your only customer. So what, are those hallway cameras just supposed to collect dust?"

Even with that stroke of luck, even though the janitor wouldn't be able to prove his attackers weren't squirrels, Marco knew he'd have to figure something out. As the day had proven, he couldn't keep the monsters in his desk all day. But he couldn't leave them at home either. *They'll get bored, and who knows what kind of trouble they'll get into? Plus, the whole point of having monsters was to show them off at school.*

But that's not *their whole point,* Marco corrected himself. He widened the flaps of his backpack. His monsters looked up and grinned big, toothy grins. "You're my friends, and I want you around," Marco said, making them smile bigger.

After his ride home with his mom, him reassuring her he just needed some rest, Marco entered his room with a feeling that he should check his phone. Because *maybe* there'd be more chatter on it than usual.

In fact, his phone was blowing up with texts—had *been* blowing up since he revealed his monsters. But, as usual, his phone was home and silenced, so he was unaware. It took him about two seconds to decide, *nope, not gonna spend the whole evening answering a hundred texts.* Instead, he shot off a quick message to Jimena, la informadora, the queen of gossip. Sharing news with *her* was faster than any social media.

Nothing bad happened. I'm fine. We'll be at school tomorrow.

We meaning him and his monsters. And he was determined to make it so.

He set down his phone and got planning.

Chapter 16

Hidden Access

Marco made sure to take so long getting ready in the morning that he was late for school and his mom had to drive him in. That would make her late too, and he felt bad about that.

"No te preocupes, nene," she said when he apologized. Her eyes flicked to the rearview mirror to meet his in the back seat. "Don' worry. I'm glad jou feelin better today." She was wearing a light blue dress with pink heels and held a tumbler decorated with smaller tumblers like itself. An infinite loop of coffee. His mother's dream. At the red light, she took a sip and smacked her lips. "Maite came to da house las' night, mijo, asking for jou but I sent her home."

Marco's backpack pitched in the back seat, and he patted it, hoping the monsters would be still.

They told him yesterday how the janitor seeing them made them panic.

"I told her jou was just na feeling good, and she say she'll see jou at school. She's a sweet girl, mijo, to check to see if jou okay."

Marco felt his heart trip a little. "Yeah, she sure is sweet, Mami."

"She makes me think, I no see Tinker in a long time. Jou two okay?"

Marco deflated. "We haven't been getting along this year, Mami."

Her eyes flicked to the rearview mirror and held for just a second before returning to the road. In that second, she managed to send a lot of care. "No sé lo que pasó entre ustedes, chiquito, pero no te olvides: amistades que son verdaderas mantengan sus puertas abiertas."

Marco swallowed. No, she didn't know what was going on between them, and she was sweet to call him Little One, but her advice stung, even though she didn't mean it to. She reminded him of a saying he'd forgotten. *Friendships that are true keep their doors open.* He nodded before turning to the window to think.

"Jou migh no have recess today, mi amor. Veo nubarrones."

He saw them too. Storm clouds ahead.

When she parked in front of the school, Marco leaned forward to kiss her on the cheek. "Gracias, Mamita." She smiled like he was the sun.

He pulled out his backpack and another bag and headed into school. His mom had called ahead to excuse his tardiness. This late arrival would provide exactly what he needed from the main office: a hall pass, that magical token that bestows exquisite, delicious freedom to roam.

With the pass in hand, Marco hurried toward the drama department's prop room, a long, narrow room behind the stage wall. On the other side of the wall was the raised stage that formed the short end of the rectangular lunch room. The prop room was perfect for Marco's plans. It was theatrical, mostly unused, and in a loud area. The K-1st grade classes were next door.

Standing in front of the prop room door, Marco pulled a key from his pocket. He felt a twinge of guilt that he still had it. He should've returned it to Ms. Mira after last spring's school play put on by the 7th and 8th graders, but he forgot. He was in and out of that room so much during lunch, recess, and before and after school that Ms. Mira simply gave him a key to save herself the trouble of escorting him in. Now it was the perfect home base for monsters.

Marco quickly unlocked the door, stepped in, and re-locked it behind him. He hit the light switch and turned to see a glorious artistic mess. Lining the walls were shelves loaded with odd artifacts from past productions. The center of the room was cluttered with wooden scenery slabs, banner tubes, boxes overflowing with clothes and fabric, and long fanning feathers.

GGM's upper grades put on a show every other year. Last year, Ms. Mira had Marco paint the complicated set pieces, while a few other 5th graders painted simpler pieces. The school wouldn't host a show this year, which would've normally made him sad. But not now.

"Compinches, buddies, welcome to your home away from home." Marco set one backpack on the floor. Camo, Stinky, and Growler crawled out and slowly spun on their heels, taking it all in. "This is the room I mentioned last night. Our secret lair. Cool, right? You can play or rest or grab a snack so you don't get bored. But first, give me a minute."

He heaved his other, bigger bag off his shoulder to thud to the ground. He quickly prepared the space. He lowered some stacked boxes to the floor so they wouldn't topple. He laid fabric across the base of an old dog house used in a production about a flying beagle and set one of his dirty T-shirts from the bag onto the fabric so his monsters would have a safe place to hide that smelled like him and brought them comfort. He put another dirty T-shirt on a shelf, partly hidden by feather fans, for another hiding spot. His final tee he wrapped around the bottom rung of a ladder he propped against the wall leading to an air vent. The T-shirt would make the ladder less scary and encourage Growler to climb the metal rather than claw his way up walls.

The rest of the backpack was filled with snacks. There were granola bars, fruit cups, whole apples, mildly squished bananas, chip bags, and three peanut-butter-and-jelly sandwiches. He hid the food within a series of shallow serving bowls created for a production of Cleopatra. Marco had fun hand painting hieroglyphs on the sides. His monsters watched him intently. "Try to make this food last until lunch at least." Camo flashed green in response.

Finally, Marco pulled toys from every pocket of his cargo shorts. He had tiny plastic cars, bouncy balls, a mini-slinky, a full-sized Rubik's cube, a keychain stuffed bear he noticed Camo had taken a liking to, Stinky's favorite army men, and Growler's Stretch Armstrong. He hid the toys around the room so they'd know where their toys were, but no one else would.

"Growler," Marco said, "your awesome idea to use air shafts to travel around the school will let you see what's happening in a lot of different rooms, not just mine, so you won't get bored. But remember, inside the air ducts, you need to be quiet." He watched his monsters separate to start exploring the room. "I hope you love it here. See you later."

With that, he left for Music class, where Ms. Mira was introducing the class to salsa—the music, not the food. "This is a güiro." She held aloft one of Marco's favorite instruments and scraped a stick over its grooves. "The güiro was created in Puerto Rico and was so popular, it spread to surrounding areas and became the distinctive sound of Latin American music. We'll spend 15 minutes making our own, and then we'll play them."

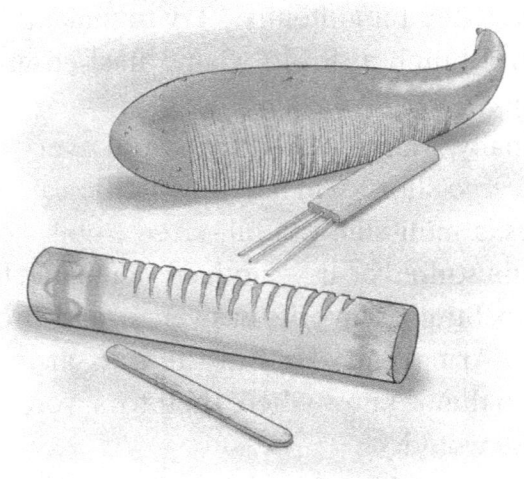

Marco had a traditional güiro at home. It was made by hollowing a long gourd, cutting thumb-and-finger holes on one side, carving grooves on the other, then letting the whole thing dry hard. Marco's güiro had the classic metal comb to scrape across the grooves and scratch a beat. Ms. Mira's idea for homemade güiros worked too, though. "I've shortened some wooden dowels," she said, passing out wooden cylinders about eight inches long and an inch wide. "Use these metal files to gouge some grooves." The files looked like magic wands. Soon the *sssshhh, sssshhh* sound of groove-making overcame the silence.

Marco thought about the Mexican version of the güiro, the quijada. Marco nearly lost his mind with envy when he learned it was made from the dried jawbone of a donkey. *How gross is that? The* donkey decays and its gums retract, so its teeth loosen in the jaw. Musicians making a beat either scraped a stick across the teeth or shook the whole jawbone like a maraca.

Ms. Mira soon handed out popsicle sticks for kids to scrape across their güiro's ridges. She turned up the music and called out, "¡A tus pies! Dance if you'd like!"

Every chair scraped. Kids rose, happy to move. Marco, from the back of the room, eyed Tinker at the front. His mom's words floated back to him.

Friendships that are true keep their doors open. That requires two *open doors,* he thought, *but maybe it wouldn't hurt to try.*

First, though, he shimmied toward the air vent, knowing all the noise would attract his monsters. *There they are.* Three tiny pairs of eyes at the vent blinked and hands waved hello. He was about to wave back when the classroom door burst open and the janitor charged in.

But he wasn't just charging in. The janitor was charging *him*. Marco felt his eyes widen and his feet turn to ice as he froze on the spot. When the janitor reached him, the short but surprisingly strong man grabbed Marco's shoulders and yanked him aside.

"Mr. Sanders! You cannot interrupt class, much less touch students." The school principal came in hot on the janitor's heals. "There are no monsters in this building! You experienced a traumatic fright, is all!"

"I set some mirrors in the ductwork, and I'm telling ya I saw something move in this direction. Ach, move aside, boy!"

Marco didn't dare look up. He sure hoped everyone up there would know to run.

"You set mirrors in the duct work?!" asked Principal Álvaro. "That has got to be a fire code violation." She reached Mr. Sanders and stood over him—she was noticeably taller— forcing him to pull his eyes away from the vent and onto her. "Mr. Sanders, kindly leave this classroom, remove any and all mirrors from vents, and report to my office. We'll discuss exactly what it was you saw and what can be done about it. It'll be all right."

Her tone had an edge of "*we* will do nothing about your imagination and *you* will get ahold of yourself." *Or maybe that's wishful thinking,* Marco mused. It was only then he noticed the music had stopped. Ms. Mira's hand was paused over her phone, and all eyes were trained on him, as if *he'd* stopped the music and fun. He shrugged, like, *what was that all about?*

After the bell rang and the line leader escorted students into the hall, Marco stayed back to tell Ms. Mira he wanted to start an art club. "Espléndido, Marco. I'll help you fill the club request form during the next Art class. Now please go catch the line."

When Marco stepped into the hall, he found Tinker standing dead center, splitting the lines of kids to either side of him, like a boulder parting a river. He held a red paper in his hand. Marco knew he didn't have a hall pass, but he deeply admired the faking of it.

"Maybe you'd like to explain things over lunch," Tinker said. "Like how you made monsters and if you're going to keep disrupting school with them."

Marco really, really, really wanted to say, "Or maybe I won't explain a thing" or, "*I* didn't stop class today." But *not* explaining anything wouldn't be fair to Rosita, who really did deserve to know why Marco was going to sit someplace else at lunch that day.

"Sure," Marco answered. The tension between them prickled, and each walked toward the lunchroom skimming the hall's opposite walls, putting as much distance between themselves as possible.

Chapter 17

Salami on Rye

"Why're you sitting here?" Rosita asked after Marco settled in at the table closest to the raised stage. She waved everyone over as if they'd all instantly want to sit wherever he did. Tinker was already there, sitting across from him, arms crossed, eyes all squinty and hostile. Maite and Knox followed Rosita's lead and sunk onto the bench seats. Knox looked like he did it unwillingly.

"Have you two made up?" Rosita asked, looking at Marco and Tinker in turn. "'Cause this has been the longest fight I've ever seen."

"It's been two and a half weeks," Maite said, "That's, like, a school record. How stubborn are you two?"

Marco and Tinker met eyes, and for a fraction of a second Marco thought he saw in them what he himself was thinking, that if he was going to hold a record at that school, "longest fight" wasn't the prize he'd want.

Knox snort-laughed. "It's Marco who's being stubborn."

"I heard both sides, and it's both their faults." Maite replied. "Tinker should have been more forgiving of Marco missing their meetup, and Marco should have kept his promise plus not un-invited him from the art club he wants to start."

"So Marco did two things wrong to Tinker's one," Knox countered. "You'd stop defending Marco if he wasn't being extra nice to you. He's playing you."

"Wait just a second," Maite said and raised to stand.

Oh, snap.

"People can be nice to me without it fooling me," Maite said, her voice now rising just as she had risen to stand. "And are you saying I can't think straight when people are nice to me?" Marco noticed she was catching the attention of nearby tables.

Knox raised both hands to make just-calm-down pats to the air.

Ooh, bad move.

"I'm saying he's not being nice *just* to be nice."

"What would *you* know about being nice?" Maite said, catching the attention of Señor Ortiz, their Science, Social Studies, and Health teacher and their lunchroom monitor for the day.

Marco definitely didn't want this topic to go on. He didn't want *his* fight with Tinker to radiate and cause more. *Plus, if Maite gets any louder, the lunch ladies will hear her even through their hair nets.* Marco quickly thought how grateful he was when food-people wore hair nets. No matter, attention toward this side of the lunchroom was *bad*.

"Let's just drop it," Knox said in a huff, crossing his arms and looking away.

The silence that followed was awful. Everyone chose to quietly dig into their lunch rather than risk another blow-up. Marco hated that this whole thing was pitting friends, even family, against each other. Plus, he had to admit, when Maite listed the reasons behind their fight, his column *did* have two marks to Tinker's one. *But Tink did boss me around at the junkyard*, he told himself, adding another item to Tink's list of offenses. Still, all that did was make the fight equally their faults. *Maybe no one was in the right here.*

Marco felt ... conflicted.

Ten minutes later, he heard scratching behind him. He swiveled to look into the crisscrossed wooden grate that formed the front face of the stage. Through a gap he pushed a rolled up pizza slice wrapped in a napkin. Growler snatched it.

"Wow! There they are!" Rosita said, way too loud. "I wondered why you didn't bring them today, but Maite told me not to bring it up in case you got in trouble for them."

Maite rolled her eyes.

"So, you're feeding them?" Rosita stretched her neck trying to see them better.

Tinker half stood to peer over the table.

"Yep," Marco said, then added, "They need to eat, Rosita, just like us. And they play and do just about anything else we do. They're awesome."

Camo came to the grate and waved to Rosita. Rosita waved back.

It wasn't long before a few kids walked over to their table. Then more. Marco urged them to sit, not point, don't alert the adults. He knew these kids were gravitating toward him out of curiosity and not because Marco was suddenly popular or anything—*I mean, the monsters may make me seem popular, but they're the stars.* Still, he noticed Tinker listen hard to every question they lobbed. Marco decided the previous night how he'd answer randos.

"What can they do?"

"I can't say."—Truth. He'd only had them a few days. How could he know?

"How are they alive?"

"I can't say."—Truth. *Maybe I should know, but I'm not fired up enough yet to find out. Besides, how is anything alive?*

"Where did you get them?"

That was the most popular question. And though Marco *could* say, he wasn't dumb enough to do so. Last week, he wanted monsters to make Tinker jealous, to make Tink see how cool he was with new friends, and if Tink had all the answers to their mysteries, well, he wouldn't be quite as impressed. The other reason Marco wouldn't say where he got the monsters was because he knew they weren't asking out of simple curiosity. They wanted their own. So, while it wasn't entirely true to say "I can't say," it was true that he couldn't say *at that moment* because saying so would lose them part of their magical appeal. *No one else has monsters, and I need this.* With Tinker being super hostile and Knox bullying him, he needed friends, someone he could talk to and play with so he wouldn't feel quite so alone.

His eyes met Tinker's and held them, not in a mean way. He figured that now that Tink could see the monsters were 100 percent real and had replaced him as bestie, maybe it was time to take a little risk, open the door of true friendship. Marco put a cookie into a napkin and reached across the table to offer it to Tinker. "Would you like to feed them?"

Tinker dropped his fork with a clang. "Let me get this straight," he said. "You show up with your 'new,' friends, some fake animated junk or trained pets or whatever, who you loudly insinuate are better than your real friends. You show them off, make three huge scenes so far, get loads of attention, probably hoping to butter up kids and add them to your 'friend' list, and then you want me to—what? Play along? Love on your pets? Act like we're still buddies? Like nothing's wrong? Don't you think you should instead work on making true friends?"

This reaction wasn't what Marco expected. At all. What did Tinker want from him? To curl up and die after their friendship imploded? Was he not supposed to move on? Was he supposed to just *take* this talk? Especially after the peace offering of a cookie? After a heartbeat, he decided he had something to say too. "Don't you think *you* should work on friendship?"

Tinker stood agog before snatching his tray and storming back to their old table. Knox shot Marco a look of disgust, the kind of look you might give a waiter after finding a cockroach in the pasta. He followed Tinker. Rosita and Maite looked at each other. They seemed as lost as Marco, who had hoped, at first, to be seen as the peacemaker, a gentleman. He expected the single, generous act of sharing a moment with his monsters to be seen as selfless compromise.

Nope. Marco sighed. "Sit where you'd like," he told the girls. He wasn't about to orchestrate a war.

"Obviously," Maite said, before whispering to Rosita and leaving to follow her brother.

Rosita stayed. "She doesn't want to fight anymore with Knox."

"I understand. Thanks for staying with me, Rosi."

He was about to hand her the cookie he had offered Tink when Mrs. Kroppert appeared at his side, casting a shadow over his food and life. He heard a small scuttle behind him and hoped the monsters had retreated into the grate's shadows.

"Hi," Rosita chirped to his teacher. She patted the bench. "Want to sit with us?"

Wut. Marco resisted the urge to drop his face into his hands. *Rosita, how could you?* Being two years younger meant she didn't know Mrs. Kroppert, but being only one grade behind Marco meant he'd tell her, prepare her for what was coming. He'd loved all his teachers so far, but Mrs. Kroppert? *You don't sit with her unless you're okay with her spying on your kid drama and finding out who's friends with who but still ignoring your problems when you ask for help.* Mrs. Kroppert was the last person Marco would go to again.

"No, thank you, young lady," Mrs. Kroppert answered.

Pfft, does she even know Rosita's name?

"Several teachers have lost their lunch."

Rosita giggled and put a hand over her mouth.

"I mean to say, their lunches were taken. The teacher's lounge was littered with sandwich bags and chip wrappers, and the culprits apparently thought it would be funny to lay out peels from all the bananas they ate. We're looking for kids not eating. Or food that's...familiar."

Marco's eyes flashed across the lunchroom and over the six or seven teachers who suddenly appeared in the room like roaming ghosts, drifting and weaving around tables, peering at food trays. He wondered how they'd be able to tell which carrot sticks might be theirs? Or how it could possibly be fair to punish someone for not eating. *What if they've finished?* And who would dare go into the teacher's lounge? Much less trust their food?

A loud, long burp erupted behind him, trailing into a growl, followed by a high-pitched squeal. Marco's stomach dropped. *OMG.* He looked to Rosita, who—*gracias al cielo*—knew exactly what to do. She cackled as high pitched as Camo and slapped her knee for added measure.

"Mr. Torres, kindly excuse yourself." Mrs. Kroppert frowned at him from on high, towering above him as both judge and executioner. "And you, young lady, you mustn't encourage such brute behavior."

Mustn't? Did she say mustn't? What century are we in? Marco and Rosita locked eyes, and her cackle instantly went wild. She dissolved into the kind of kid-laugh where breathing goes raspy and cheeks burn pink. Mrs. Kroppert, on the other hand, raged red.

"Just what. Is so. Funny. Little miss?"

Oh no, the bark. The dramatics. Time to intervene.

"She's got the giggles, Mrs. Kroppert. Sorry about that. And, yes." Marco dabbed the corners of his mouth with his paper napkin like a prince at court. "Please do excuse me."

Rosita honked, she laughed so hard.

Mrs. Kroppert's frowned deepened. Her mouth was now a perfect upside U. An archway of anger. Omega intersected. Whatever it was, it wasn't good.

"I hope. You're not. Mocking me. Mr. Torres."

"Oh no, Mrs. Kroppert. I hope you find your lunch." He pushed his lunch tray toward her, ostensibly offering his pizza, with one slice rolled in a napkin for a monster, handled and bent and oozing grease. Rosita nearly fell off her seat laughing.

Mrs. Kroppert's eyes flicked from Marco's tray to his face.

Guau, está esperando que yo me ría. But he wouldn't crack and laugh. He kept his face perfectly neutral, as quiet as he imagined a face could look.

"I prefer my own lunch. You two do understand that any student aware of thieving is complicit in the act?"

"What's—what's—?" Rosita couldn't even talk.

I've never seen her like this. Marco barely held on.

"Complicit means they're just as guilty. If you hear who it was who entered the teacher's lounge and helped themselves to *our* meals, you are to report it." Mrs. Kroppert nodded a curt goodbye and walked to the next table, stalking for a thief.

When he was sure her attention was elsewhere, Marco spun on his seat and hissed into the grate, "No me digas, don't you tell me, that you took the teachers' lunches."

Stinky burped in response, much lower-pitched than Growler and rising at the end like a question. Marco knew what the question was, too—*Do you want us to* not *tell you? OR do you want to know how much we enjoyed their salami on rye?*

Marco waved a hand in front of this nose. *Oof, definitely salami on rye.*

"Colegas, we'll talk about this tonight." He said it softly but still didn't like how it sounded, like it was laced in threat, so he added, "Don't worry, I'm not mad."

Still, he spent the rest of lunch keeping an eye on teachers and handing Rosita food wrapped in napkins to slip to the monsters. Because they were still hungry. Of course they were. *I'll have to bring extra snacks tomorrow.* Rosita never looked happier. She handed Camo a sugar cookie and the pair held hands through the grate.

Besides watching the teachers, he also occasionally flicked his eyes toward Tinker, but at no point did Tinker look his way. *So much for opening a door. And the thing about opening a door,* Marco realized, *is that once you do, you really want someone to walk through. Or walk through yourself. Because now you've opened yourself up a bit.*

That night, Marco pulled from his nightstand the photo of himself and Tink, the one he'd bent in half to get Tink out of sight. He unfolded it and stared at his ex-bestie a long time before reluctantly bending it back.

Chapter 18

The Keys to Trouble

The next morning, Marco explained to Growler, Camo, and Stinky that just because *he* shares everything doesn't mean *everyone* wants to. He intended to bring it up last night after dinner, but they looked so well fed and happy spinning their spirograph cogs that he couldn't spoil their fun. *What's a few more hours? I'll talk to them in the morning, so it's fresh in their minds.*

Finishing his last bite of breakfast, he ended the talk with, "La gente se fastidia, and annoyed people take steps we won't want them to. So don't take anything else, okay?"

The monsters' eyes met in a way that made the hair on Marco's arms stand up.

He rubbed his temple, almost afraid to ask. "What now?"

Camo crawled into his backpack and pulled out a big silver keyring holding 20 or so keys. They jingled. She mimicked the sound and turned herself silver as a bell.

Two thoughts popped into Marco's mind. First, *How did I not hear keys jingling on the walk home yesterday?* But he quickly answered his own question. He had three furry friends squished into a pretty tight space, and whatever they sat on wouldn't bounce. The second thought was, *Who do these belong to? Or, as Mrs. Kroppert would say, To whom do these belong?* He shook his head. Mrs. K might not be his favorite, but her teachings sure stuck in his brain.

He reached for the large loop and turned it over in his hand. White words sprawled over a metal decoration of a red brick schoolhouse: "Montse Álvaro, Principal, Gabriel García Márquez K-8." One of the keys had a black plastic head. A car key. The rest were for doors.

Marco didn't blink. Lost all ability to think rationally. *Is it possible to keel over and die from fear?* He guessed it was. *People talk all the time about dying from fright. And maybe a quick death is better than the my-life-is-over punishment coming if I'm caught with these keys.*

He pictured getting to school that morning, stepping through the front door, and having his bag snatched and searched. He'd be dragged by the ear to the principal's office. *Do they still do that, drag people by their ears? That's gotta be really bad for ears. Señora Álvaro will be shocked that such a good boy as me had stolen her keys. She'll rant and rail about what a loss of trust I've committed, how dangerous it is for others to have keys. She'll call my folks. Then the police. And I'll have to explain to the judge that it was me, I stole the keys, because there's no way I'll nark on my monsters 'cuz they'll get shipped off to some spy lab somewhere and I'll never see them again. I'll be found guilty, after my confession, and I'll go to jail forever and ever and ever, and it'll break Mami's and Papi's hearts. And mine too. I want to be an artist. I don't want to spend my life pounding license plates in jail.*

Marco was frozen so long that it was only when Stinky sprawled across his face, hugging him and telling him, "Wake up! Wake up!" that Marco snapped to.

I. Am. In. Trouble.

"Buddies, this is bad. Why did you take these?"

"Lady use keys to open doors," Stinky said with a shrug. "Some rooms no have vents."

"You took the keys to access rooms that didn't have vents?" He felt a spike of fury. They had access to nearly the entire building. They certainly saw things he never had, got into rooms he couldn't. *Yet it wasn't enough?* Their curiosity would cost him dearly if he got caught with stolen keys. But he looked at their hopeful faces peering up at him with concern and knew he couldn't stay angry with them. *They're just curious and don't know any better.*

"We'll fix this."

A half hour later he approached the school on foot and still hadn't formulated a solid plan. He knew he couldn't risk walking through the front door with his monsters. *If my classmates don't give them away, the dragnet might.* He pictured a line of teachers searching backpacks for stolen booty. Then he saw the solution to his problems. There, just right there, was a tree, a perfect tree, as most are, but this particular beauty, this savior, grew at a corner of the school, making it super unlikely anyone inside could see it. Teachers usually placed low bookshelves in front of windows to allow in a breeze while preventing anyone from sticking their head out. That meant they couldn't get an angled view to, say, a corner tree. *Yippee kie-yay.* He plopped down at its base, out of sight of the main doors, and casually opened his backpack.

"Up and in, colegas," he said. "Stay on this side of the trunk. And return those keys."

He watched Camo duck her head into the keyring, making a techy necklace of the whole thing, before the monsters clambered up and leapt into an open window. *Whew.*

Marco peeked around the trunk to the main doors, making sure he was in the clear before standing. He slung his empty backpack over one shoulder and sauntered to the main entrance looking as innocent as any other kid. But he wasn't, so it came as little surprise a half hour later when the classroom speaker crackled to life and the principal asked students to be on the lookout for her keyring, which she must have dropped yesterday somewhere on the grounds.

"That ring has important keys for the school," Señora Álvaro said. "It's for your safety that you hand them in at the office if you come across them. But you should know the school is safe. I stayed here overnight to make sure no one came in who didn't belong."

Oh. Marco looked at his hands. *She didn't have her car keys. She could have called someone for a ride, but she didn't. Huh. She refused to leave the building insecure.*

Marco felt crummy, especially when it occurred to him that she didn't accuse anyone of thievery the day after teachers' lunches were definitely pilfered. *Or maybe she* knows *her keys were stolen and will blame whoever hands them in.* He looked up from his hands to see his entire class turned his way, Tinker included. He felt his ex-bestie's eyes burning into him.

Unfortunately, Mrs. Kroppert caught on. "Marco, do you have anything to say?"

Boy howdy, the room was warm. On fire, almost. "Uh, I'd say Señora Álvaro should check her office. It's usually messy. Maybe look under a pile of papers." He heard shuffling overhead, his monsters arriving and getting comfortable or taking off, expecting trouble.

"It is not. For you. Mr. Torres. To comment on. The cleanliness of an office."

"Sorry, Mrs. Kroppert."

For the next half hour, he was distracted by the janitor and those teachers who must have had a free period walk past his open door, hunched and looking down. *Why are they still looking for the keys?* Hadn't he told his monsters to return them? When a white rabbit hopped past, he knew what happened even before the announcement confirmed it.

"Attention, student body. Someone—or perhaps several someones—has freed the school's pets. We have discovered ten empty cages. They housed three rabbits, two turtles, two hamsters, two guinea pigs, and one bearded dragon. If you see these animals, please do not approach them, as it may scare them. Get the attention of a grownup and let them handle it."

All eyes turned his way but Marco couldn't meet them. He stared ahead, scared out of his mind. *What are they* doing*?! My monsters can't think this is right.* A scuttle overhead drew his—and everyone else's—eyes upward. Staring down at him through the vent above, was a yellow-orange bearded dragon. It blinked as if thanking him for its freedom.

A scream pierced the quiet, followed by, "Drago-o-o-o-o-n!"

Mrs. Kroppert hustled out of the room to shout down the hall for the janitor. He was there within seconds, promising to catch it—and anything else— in the air ducts.

By lunchtime, six of the animals had been recaptured but none from the air ducts. The bearded dragon remained on the loose. The whole morning, Marco silently hoped that his monsters would lay low, stay hidden, not get caught. But in the lunchroom, just as he was working to thread a juice box into the lair grate, he was surprised to see Stinky not behind it but right at his feet. "Whoa! What are you doing out here?"

Camo answered. "Teachers looking for keys aren't looking for us." She stepped out of the grate through a small hole in the corner. Rosita slid under the table and hugged her.

"Wait, so you haven't returned the keys yet?"

"Soon," she answered, snuggling in to Rosita's embrace.

Disgusted, Marco looked for Growler. He wasn't behind the lair grate. He wasn't under their table. *Where is he?* He stood and caught a dismaying glimpse of him under the table two tables down. A 4th-grader he didn't know squealed and raised his feet before the kid next to him clapped a hand over his mouth. After the squealer calmed down, the mouth clapper whispered, and they both lowered food to their frightening visitor.

Whut is happening? Marco asked himself. *How could I lose control so badly?*

"Aw, Marco, they wanna meet more kids," Rosita said, apparently reading the dismay on his face. "Don't worry. They're okay."

She sounded an awful lot like a teacher reassuring a new parent sending their kid off to school for the first time. *They'll be scared at first, but they'll make new friends and then wonder how they ever went without them. Please don't worry.* But he was worried, not that they'd abandon him—he was pretty sure they had a strong bond, one forged in bathwater—but he wasn't ready to just...share them yet. *They're* my *monsters. Not those fourth-graders' monsters.*

He looked toward Tinker and Knox and Maite, and the feeling intensified. *Is this—could it be—jealousy?* He frowned. He didn't like Tink being so newly friendly with Knox. And he always missed Maite whenever she chose not to hang with him. *Still,* he realized with a sigh, *Rosita's right. I can't keep my monsters hiding in air ducts and behind grates forever. I don't want to imprison them. Isn't that exactly what I worried about from adults?*

Stinky drifted off to other tables too, releasing a drool-inducing smell of tacos behind him. He and Growler could handle themselves, Marco realized, in small groups. Kids seated at tables didn't get grabby like the mob on the sidewalk when he'd revealed them. His monsters accepted food from some people and held their hand while they ate. Other hands they slapped, rejecting whatever food was offered. Marco couldn't see any reasoning behind it. More importantly, they avoided the distracted gaze of the single lunchroom monitor. All the other teachers, Marco realized, were scrambling to find pets. The adults were really off their game without those keys. *Camo's brilliant.*

Two hours later, Mr. Grimm tested his PhysEd class with a timed run. GGM didn't have a track, so the kids would run around the block three times. The fast runners stood at the line. Slower kids started farther back so the fasties wouldn't trample them. It made sense to Marco, but he also though the staggered start was another way gym class wasn't exactly *encouraging*. He thought to last year, when a few kids got their gym grade knocked down because they couldn't do 25 sit-ups in a minute even though they showed improvement. Other students who easily did 25 sit-ups, no sweat, got an instant A. *So unfair.*

Mr. Grimm raised his whistle, snapping Marco to attention. At the trill, he and his fast pack took off from the line. Marco just turned the first corner when he spotted his monsters sprinting toward the sidewalk to join in.

Santos cielos, what are they doing?! "Go back!" he shouted.

But they didn't. They ran their little legs off. Foolishly! Out in the open!

"Done feeding school zoo," Stinky gasped. His long, yellow mane and leathery armpit hair flowed behind him as he ran, as did Growler's tentacles. Camo was just a blur. They all three jumped into the center of the group and easily kept pace.

"Aha! I knew your monsters were involved!" someone huffed from behind. "They let loose all the classroom pets."

"You don't know that. You just know that they fed them. So shut up with your suspicions because my teacher canceled a quiz to look for them, and I, for one, am pretty grateful."

Marco gulped. Ugh, it was fine, he supposed, that some good came from lost keys and freed pets. *But poor Señora Álvaro. I don't want her to spend another night here. And the pets really would be safer in their cages.* Yet he had to admit, Camo was right again. Teachers were still looking inside, freeing his monsters to safely join him in a run and burn off some energy.

"Don't worry, everybody," Marco said. "We'll enlist my friends to find and return them." He looked down to his little pals, who peered up without breaking stride. "Right, compinches?"

Growler let out a huff before agreeing. "Okay."

The running pack seemed to enjoy the monster company, judging by the "Ooh, you're fast" and "Nice stride" and "Come run by me." The pack even grew as slower kids sprinted with all their might to join and gawk and holler for as long as they could hold on. To any teacher watching, the students merely stuck together because they kept a similar pace, and wasn't it nice that they encouraged each other? They wouldn't be able to see the small figures at the kids' feet, thanks to the blur of so many feet in motion.

Marco felt his chest expand. His monsters were out in the open, kids accepting them. He felt less lonely than he had in weeks. He lifted his face to the sun to soak up the moment, but it didn't last long. After two laps, at the final corner, just before re-entering Mr. Grimm's line of sight, Marco had to tell his monsters to peel away. He watched, smiling, as they galloped toward the school, leaving behind calls of "Thanks for running with us" shouted in their wake. They bounded up the tree and vaulted into the window.

A second later, he heard Camo scream.

Chapter 19

The Slammer

It wasn't a normal sound, not the kind of playful shout Marco was used to. No, this was all surprise and fear. When he looked up, he saw human hands slam the window shut, then Camo claw against it.

Marco bolted from the pack. Maybe Mr. Grimm wouldn't notice his absence as other kids rounded the turn and sprinted to finish. Or maybe he would. Marco didn't care. He tore to the tree his monsters had climbed before realizing he wouldn't be able to follow them that way. *Stupid, stupid, stupid!* He hurtled along the brick wall to the front of the school. Mr. Grimm stood at the sidewalk with his back turned, shouting times to finishers. Amazingly, no one pointed to Marco or ratted him out. *Allies, finally!*

He barreled into the school and down the hallway and up the stairs and had just rounded a bend when his feet tangled with something and he tripped, sprawling, skidding on his belly until the burn of palms against tiles stopped his momentum. He heard them squeak too, his palms, the skin rasping against the flooring. *That's gonna leave a mark.*

He whipped around to see what he'd tripped on. Camo materialized out of nowhere, police siren red and flashing. Growler landed beside her as if swinging from the ceiling. Marco looked up and spotted electrical wiring bowed lower than it should be.

"What happened?" Marco asked just as Camo shouted, "He trapped Stinky!"

"What? Who?"

"The closet man, he mirrored up our tunnels and put a pretty cupcake in a cage. When I went in, he jumped out from nowhere to close it. But I became the cage. And I escaped. Stinky didn't see. He opened the door and ran in to help. Now he's stuck."

"Monster!"

Marco recognized the voice.

"Principal Álvaro, I caught one!"

Marco slammed himself against the wall as Camo seemed to disappear. Growler ran up a locker and scrambled his way to the ceiling. The janitor burst out of a room to run past, seemingly not noticing him.

"I got tha proof! There's monsters in dis school!"

Proof?! Marco watched as Mr. Sanders descended the stairs he'd just run up. He stood immobile until a hard slap rattled his teeth.

"Stinky's trapped!" Camo shouted.

Marco snapped to and sprinted to the room where Mr. Sanders had emerged. When he burst in, he found a cage on the floor with a cupcake and Stinky inside. His monster was a jailbird, pulling on the bars. Marco ran and yanked the door, shaking the cage and rocking Stinky like he was caught in an earthquake. Worse, Stinky slipped and slid on his own panicked slime.

"I can't open it!" Marco pulled and twisted. If he didn't free his friend soon, they'd both be found out. Both trapped. Both in trouble. A sudden thought broke through. "Camo! Keys!"

"Wait here!" She seemed to dematerialize on the spot.

The air shimmied with the scent of hamster cage.

"Not now, Stinky!"

"But maybe fool Principi!"

"Nothing'll fool the principal if you're found here like this. You think she'll smell hamsters and mistake you for one? This is serious! Can't you squeeze out?"

Stinky rammed himself against the bars, not making a dent, much less pushing his way through, just as Camo rematerialized in the doorway with the keyring across her chest. Growler dropped to the floor beside her from the ceiling above, wrangling something wiggly and thrashing. It took Marco a second to recognize it as one of the school's missing class pets, the most exotic, interesting, and fastest moving one. Growler had his arms wrapped around its middle, trying to contain it despite its flailing tail.

"Yes!" Marco shouted. "Quick!" His moves took a fraction of a second.

"I caught it, Montse!" returned the voice from the hall. Footfalls grew closer, accompanied with shouts of, "Impossible" and "Tom, this is buffoonery!"

"Here it is, Montse," The janitor shouted, rushing past the door and waving Sra. Álvaro in. "The monster I told you abou—" He stopped so abruptly that Sra. Álvaro collided into him and Mrs. Kroppert into her.

"It'ssss," Mr. Sanders said slowly, his voice trailing, "a dragon?"

Sra. Álvaro and Mrs. Kroppert shared a look as they recognized the school's one and only lizard, its yellow-orange bearded dragon. Mrs. Kroppert lifted a hand to her temple. Sra. Álvaro straightened her back.

"Tom." The principal addressed him with authority.

"But—but— I caught a monster, and it was real, and—"

"Mr. Sanders." The principal cut through his stammering. "Your. Vacation. Starts. Now.

She spun on her heels and left the room, followed by Mrs. Kroppert and the janitor, who trailed behind, uselessly pleading his case. Marco rose from under the teacher's desk where he'd hid. His pulse raced. He tried to slow his heart and lungs even as he gasped, "The bearded dragon?" Growler and Stinky came out of their own hiding spot behind a bookshelf. There was so much to ask them. *Why did you three release the pets in the first place? What did you want with them? How did you find that one right when we needed it?*

"My favorite," Growler said, himself a little out of breath. "He liked being free a while."

Ah. Of course. The monsters would want freedom for living things. They'd want to feed them, play with them, set them loose in the air ducts or the halls and cause general chaos. Thinking of chaos, he looked around. "Where's Camo?"

"She take key to principi's office." Stinky was nearly panting from fright.

"Finally," Marco said with a huff of relief.

At the end of the school day, the speaker on the class wall reanimated with Sra. Álvaro's voice thanking school staff for helping search for her keys, which she'd found. What she didn't say was that the keys were on her desk, under papers, a spot already unlikely but now proven not-an-accident based on the release of classroom pets. Someone had clearly returned them. Another thing she didn't mention was she never caught the culprits who stole her keys. And finally, she left out how she'd called a locksmith to change any lock that could be opened by a key on her ring. Marco only figured that out the next day when he entered school to the sound of hand drills and saw shiny new locks all over the place. "Also, all the school's pets have been returned to their cages."

That was Growler's doing. Marco resisted looking at Mrs. Kroppert or anyone else.

Chapter 20

Health and The Living

That next day, after the sound of hand drills faded and his classmates' general anxiety died down, Marco decided to lay low. Stay quiet. Even if it killed him. But Señor Ortiz was ticking off to his science class the characteristics of living things, and it was infuriating.

"Dey need to move—necesitan movimiento," he said, waving an arm clad in hot pink. Sr. O always wore bright colors. "Dey respond to stimuli—responden a los estímulos. An' dey need nourishment—alimento—food and water."

Okay. Camo, Stinky and Growler do all that.

"De next two traits look different for different animals—getting air and reproducing."

Getting air? Reproducing? Marco thought back to when he got them. *Small. Plasticky. Definitely not alive. Or were they? Did they have a maker or do they make themselves?* Marco didn't know, but he was sure they fell into the category of living things. *They're alive, and every kid in this school knows it.*

Even people on the internet did, though not all. Roberto showed how many doubters existed by shoving his phone in Marco's face when Sr. O wasn't looking and pointing to the comments section of a video. It had 50,000 views. Whoa.

so fake lol *yawn*
I've seen better animation in a kids' show

Good. He waved Roberto's phone away before they both got into trouble.

Trouble might find him anyway, he realized, as he picked yet another tiny wad of wet paper out of his hair. Stinky was spewing spitballs at him through a straw jutting out of the overhead grate. They were good at timing their play and staying out of sight, and even though Tinker crossed his arms, slumped in his chair, and told them to "stop distracting the class," a few kids giggled at each direct spitball-hit.

Sr. O apparently wasn't bothered by giggles during class, especially whenever the topic of reproduction came up.

Giggles probably came with the territory.

Chapter 21
The Bet

Friday, Marco could tell Tinker was up to something. His former friend glowered and slammed his desk closed more than once. Then, during lunch, he kept glancing over his shoulder and scowling at Marco and anyone else at his new table.

At recess, Tinker finally threw down the gauntlet. "All right, since you have new friends, I'll show off my new friend. I just finished him. And I bet my robot can beat your monsters any day of the week." He was being overly loud. Trying to draw attention. It was very un-Tinker-like.

The kids near them stopped whatever they were playing. They waved to others on the playground to come over, listen in, make this a thing. Marco watched them draw near.

Tink's trying to win the crowd? Fine, but everyone loves my monsters. And this scene Tink's making isn't opening any doors of friendship. Marco's earlier feelings of forgiveness evaporated. Like mist rising off a lake, a memory surfaced in Marco's mind of the two of them walking around town with their remote control trucks. Marco had shown more finesse maneuvering than Tinker had, probably thanks to his years handling a paint brush. He had a lot of manual dexterity. He found himself grinning. "All right, Tinker. A bet it is."

Tinker's eyes grew a fraction bigger, as if not expecting Marco to take up his challenge.

Marco straightened and leveled his expression. "I propose a race."

Tinker chortled. "Marco, robots don't tire. They can outpace any living creature, if that's what those monsters of yours are."

"Soooo, even though you called for a bet, you won't take it?"

Tinker's mouth tightened into a thin line, and Marco let the challenge hang in the air. He figured he had already tried breaking the ice by offering to let Tinker feed his monsters. This bet, this escalation, was all on Tinker. Besides, if he won, might Maite be impressed?

"Anyway, I don't mean a foot race," Marco went on. "I mean a race on wheels. Your robot versus one of my monsters, on our remote control trucks."

"You want...to challenge me...using something electronic?" Tinker said it as if pointing out the obvious and the stupid.

Marco noticed kids' heads swivel to follow them, their attention batted with each volley.

"Look, I'm sure you already modified your truck to make it faster or more energy efficient. I'm guessing you added nitrous oxide or magic pixie paste to increase its output. I don't care how you modified it, but bring it back to specs. And your robot can't be a *part* of the truck. The robot has to be a separate thing. Your robot and my monster will have to drive our trucks using the same remote controls we would if we were driving. Just tape the controller onto the hood or whatever. But they'll drive, not us. The challenge here is to see whether one of your robots can outdrive one of my monsters, assuming you can teach your robot to drive."

Tinker's eyes narrowed to slits. He practically hissed, "I ab-so-lute-ly can program a robot to drive."

"Well then, that's settled. Robot versus monster, on monster trucks, pedal to the metal. The first to cross the finish line shows which of us was right all along."

The crowd hooted and raised fists and jumped all around them before Tinker even had a chance to reply. They couldn't wait to see this, and Tinker would be in a bad spot if he refused.

Tinker balled his fists and leaned in. "Where and when?" he asked, pausing at each word.

The crowd froze, dying for details.

"One week from tomorrow," came a voice from the back of the crowd. A voice that always made him catch his breath. He pulled his eyes away from Tinker to see Maite push her way to the front and stand between them. "Is that enough time for you two idiots?"

Marco blew out the breath he was holding. He didn't like being called an idiot, but at least Maite was standing close to him. He pictured a calendar. *So, not* tomorrow *Saturday but* next *Saturday.* Enough time for both of them to train their proxies. He nodded. So did Tink.

"This is the stupidest way ever to settle an argument." Maite planted her fists on her hips. "But if it's what you two decide, fine. Just FINE! But *I* pick the course." She pointed her thumb at her chest, then two fingers toward them. "You two won't know where it is until the day of the race, so neither of you can practice there and gain an advantage. You'll have one week to prepare. And I'll tell you this much. I'll make the race course difficult. With obstacles and complications. I won't make it easy for you two fools to finish."

Marco wondered where the friendliness she'd shown in his room had gone.

He once again locked eyes with Tinker and could almost see in his ex-bestie's eyes the rage against him. Marco tried to emit the same energy, but his heart was squeezing with the *oh-no* feeling he sometimes got when he committed himself to something *hard*. He knew his monsters could probably learn to drive, thanks to their excellent reflexes. They could hold their own. But still, maybe a monster truck race against an *excellent* robot—because Tinker didn't do anything less than excellent—on a course of Maite's creation—when she was fed up with both of them—well, maybe this wasn't the best idea he'd ever had.

Tinker turned and walked away, without a word. Marco did the same, except he said all he needed to say that night, lying in bed with his monsters dead asleep beside him, when he reached over to his nightstand and pulled out the bent photo with Tinker. It made them look like friends. As if they'd ever been. *This photo is a lie.*

He ripped it in half, right down the middle, following the crease from the earlier fold. He hadn't thought about it beforehand and didn't regret doing it. The act reminded him of a radio show his dad sometimes listened to in the car. It was hosted by a psychologist trying to "improve the world one talk at a time." Marco remembered hearing how relationships sometimes go: first they crack, then they split.

He knew a split when he saw one.

"This?" he said out loud for the universe to hear, shaking the two halves of the photo before throwing them back into the side drawer and slamming his head back onto his pillow. "This friendship is over."

Chapter 22

Race Prep

Growler, Stinky, and Camo couldn't wait to drive. When Marco told them about the race, they jumped off his bed and hooted and hollered about how much fun it would be. He didn't tell them the race was a grudge match, and they must've been too excited to ask why he was talking again with Tinker. They just got really happy.

What did it matter, the why? Marco asked himself to clamp down a nagging sense of guilt. It took some overnight tossing and turning for him to figure out why he felt so guilty. Then he figured it out. He'd never *asked* them if they wanted to race. He just assumed they'd be okay with it. Or, maybe more truthfully, he assumed they'd take orders. *Which isn't right. Isn't that kind of why I'm ticked off with Tink, because he never considers what I might want to do?* Expecting compliance was bad enough, he thought, but denying bodily autonomy was another.

"Um, okay, so, do you want to race, mis amiguitos? Because if you don't, I can cancel the race. I mean, it doesn't mean much." *Actually, it means everything, and I'll be humiliated in front of the whole school if I back down now.* But Marco wasn't going to tell them that and force them into anything.

The monsters draped their arms over each others' shoulders and danced in a circle chanting, "Race, race, race!"

"Okay, cool. We race. Pero, oye. Hold up. I only have one truck. Tink too. So it'll just be one of you racing against one of his robots."

His monsters stopped dancing.

"But it doesn't mean you can't all learn to drive and take turns at the wheel."

His monsters hooted and bounced again in their circle.

"Maybe you'll even like a friendly competition to see who gets to be the driver."

The monsters stopped bouncing again, looked at each other, and burst out laughing.

"What's so funny?" Marco asked.

"We all the best!" Stinky said, and they hooked shoulders again and sang.

• • • ● ● • ● ● • • •

It took Marco forever to get started. He had to drag his truck out of his closet where he'd set it to dry, and that meant pulling out his plastic rolling cart with drawers full of foam bullets and plastic sheriff badges, which the monsters insisted were swords and ninja stars. That meant half an hour of play right there.

He tried to not let them see his old tin lunch box, which he was way too old for and now held a toy viewfinder, two reels, and toy airplanes. He tried to slide the tin quietly to the side, but everything inside scraped as it shifted. Stinky practically fainted when he heard it. Growler ran over and easily muscled open the rusting lid. Camo dived in, taking on the swirling patterns of reels with half of her body and the metallic shine of the planes with the other. His monsters next spotted a train. Another half hour. Then bright, bendy linking sticks, which Camo expertly blended into. When Marco pulled out a tennis racket, two monsters climbed aboard to be pulled on their sleigh. But Marco wasn't upset about the delays. The monsters made everything fun again. Finally, though, he got to his truck. He pulled it out and replaced its batteries.

"Vrooom vroom vuh vuh vuh vuh," Camo rumbled and idled in a deep voice, sounding exactly like a pulsing motor. Growler and Stinky copied her, totally into it.

The truck's cab was sealed and the windows too small for a foot-tall monster to squeeze through. But Marco knew there was room enough for a monster to sit on top. The remote control, which was the same size and shape as a video game controller, could be duct taped onto the hood, so a driver could control the truck and hold on at the same time.

Marco pulled from his closet a mini basketball that was small enough to hold upside down with one hand. He unplugged the helmet cam he got at the end of summer from his pop, who didn't like the idea of Marco taping his phone onto his RC truck. He then grabbed a bin and tossed in the basketball, a pair of scissors, his helmet cam, the truck with its controller, another controller from an old game system he didn't own anymore, a long shoelace, and some duct tape. He opened his backpack for his monsters. He had a half hour before dinner.

"¿Qué tál, hijo?" Papi asked as Marco descended the stairs.

The backpack stopped wiggling. "Nada, Papi. Afuera pa' jugar." *Just going out to "play." But actu-*

ally to teach monsters to drive. As race prep. To win neighborhood glory. No big deal.

Outside, he sat them in a half circle to watch him work. "I'm cutting an opening in the mini-basketball to make a helmet. This will protect your head and prevent friction burns from the helmet cam. I'll tie them together with a shoelace, and I'll record so we can work on technique.

"This is the truck's controller. Normally I'd use it to drive the truck down the sidewalk or over creeks or whatever, but now you'll be driving." He showed them the controls for speed and steering, saving the sound effects buttons for later. "There aren't any brakes, though, so make smart choices—or commit to your bad ones and plow through." They laughed.

He duct taped the truck's controller onto the hood and grabbed his old game controller. "I'll be pretending to steer, in case anyone spots us," he said, but he didn't care if Tinker was watching. Either of them seeing the other's driver practice wouldn't change the race's outcome, since neither was familiar with the track. "Okay, who's first?"

All three monsters pointed to another one. Marco knew they would.

"Very polite, colegas, but somebody's gotta go first." He looked them over and decided on Camo. Anyone looking out their window might not even see a monster on the truck, although they'd definitely see a floating basketball with a helmet cam on it. They'd probably think it was attached to the truck somehow. Or that their eyesight was failing. Either way, it was a chance he was willing to take. "Let's do this." He put his foot next to the truck so she could climb up easier, then strapped on the helmet and pressed record on the camera.

"Vrooom vroom vuh vuh vuh vuh," Camo said.

"You bet, hermana," Marco said, surprising himself by calling her sister. She camouflaged to look like the driveway. "Go, Camo, go!"

Guhr-ruh-ruh-ruh-ruh-rrrrrr! The monster engine roared as Camo peeled out of the driveway and whipped left onto the road. The sharp turn tilted the truck so far that it rode on two wheels for a few seconds before slamming back with a bounce onto all fours. Marco hadn't seen whether Camo had looked both ways before going into the road, but the video recording would show it. Marco made a mental note to teach safety while working on their technique.

Stinky and Growler cheered before scrambling up Marco's leg and into his backpack, peering over the top. Marco laughed out loud picturing a neighbor watching his monsters spring into the backpack. *They'll think I've got them hooked to a bungie cord or something.* But a boy running after his remote control truck was totally normal. And veering left and right, all over the road, was exceptionally normal. Nothing to see here except typical awful driving.

What wasn't funny was seeing a real pickup truck barreling toward Camo. Real, gigantic, and driven by a human. Marco's stomach leapt to his throat.

"Camo, look out!" he screamed. He watched the trucks speed toward one another—his tiny RC truck carrying one of his best friends, and a huge, two-ton machine, so tall he doubted the driver would even see Camo over its hood. He gasped as his truck, instead of veering away to safety, headed straight toward its giant twin. If Marco had been watching TV, he might have covered his eyes. A tinny police siren broke though his panic. *Camo's depending on that little sound button to clear the path?*

"Play chicken!" bellowed Growler over his shoulder.

"Jump aboard!" hollered Stinky, on the other side.

"Steer clear!" Marco screamed. He watched in horror as Camo zipped under the massive pickup and came out the other side. She tore left to rise up a driveway, spin, and face them, safely, on the sidewalk, in the direction she'd come. A disembodied mini-basketball helmet with attached video cam bobbed off and floated, as if held by the wind, next to the rumbling engine. Camo waited for them, probably leaned against the engine like a stunt-racing superhero.

Marco sprinted to her. Dropped to his knees. His monsters jumped down too. Everyone spoke at once. She reappeared in her normal multi-patterned skin.

"Camo the Brrrrrrave!" said Growler, thumping his chest.

"Mmm, you smell like burnt rubber!" Stinky told Camo while waving his hands toward his nose. "And Marco smells like fear!"

"That was terrifying," Marco said, puffing out the breath he'd been holding. When he saw her crestfallen face, he added, "Amazing too, but totally bananas, way more dangerous than it needed to be. We don't want anyone getting hurt. Wait, *can* you get hurt?"

Camo shrugged. So did the others. Marco blurted a question he'd been wondering a long time. "Do you three know where you come from? I mean, how you came to be?"

"Do you?" Camo asked. Marco frowned. *I mean, I know the basics, but maybe her question's deeper, like, where does consciousness come from.* He thought a moment before answering her with a shrug of his own. *If I can't really say, why should she?*

He refocused on race prep. "Camo, you showed good decision-making by going between the big wheels—if you didn't have options. But it's better to avoid trouble. Do what all kids do and shout 'car' when you see one coming and get off the road. Otherwise, mega cool driving."

She must've taken his praise to heart because she turned dark blue with big white stars, as if wearing a stunt motorcyclist's costume. One of the stars covered her right eye. It reminded him of a Mexican wrestling mask. He'd always wanted one. He decided right then and there to make himself one, someday, so he could be half as cool as she was in that moment, the daredevil.

"Mega cool," she said, imitating Marco and smiling before patting the truck goodbye.

Growler pulled Stinky into a bearhug. "Stinky next!"

"Sure, but the helmet may never smell the same again." Marco chuckled to himself when he realized their hugs and general closeness yielded the same results. "C'mere, bud." He bent down to outfit Stinky with the helmet while Camo and Growler climbed into the backpack. He turned the truck to face away from home and sat Stinky atop it. His greenest and yellowest monster looked both ways before taking off.

Stinky's mane was a feathery flag flying behind him. He barreled half a block down the sidewalk, holding his line straighter than Camo had, maybe because he wasn't aiming for a truck. He turned onto a yard with a kiddie play set and surged up the slide, launching over the top. The sound of laser blasters pierced the air—*pew! pew!* Stinky had hit another sound button, an exceedingly excellent one.

"Wow!" Marco shouted, waving his arms like an air-tube dancer.

Stinky and the truck floated in the air a moment before dropping and landing hard. Stinky lost hold of the truck. Everyone gasped as he bounced high, but Stinky somehow landed back on the truck, atop its rear wheel well. Since he wasn't pushing the controls to make the truck go faster, it had slowed, and Stinky crawled his way back to the roof. By the time he could reach the controller again, the truck had nearly stopped. Stinky turned it back toward the sidewalk and spun some donuts while Marco, hauling monsters, ran to his side.

"Giant juuump!" howled Growler.

"He blurred," whispered Camo, clearly impressed he went so fast he wasn't fully visible.

"That was an epic run," Marco said. "Whadya think?"

"Me smell more smells going fast," Stinky said, waving his hands toward himself and gathering all the air his nostrils could take in. He took off his helmet. Only the feathery hair plastered underneath it had stayed smooth. The rest of his mane, traveling all the way down his back, stuck straight out behind him, tangled from a wind long gone.

Growler leapt from Marco's shoulder as Stinky crawled up. He fitted the helmet and climbed the truck without help. Then he slammed his hand on the red button.

Rrrrooooaaaarrrrr! The truck trilled, loud and long.

Growler smiled and took a big breath.

"Oh no!" Marco covered his ears.

"RRRROOOOAAAARRRRR!" Growler boomed, loud enough to make bones shake.

"RRRROOOOAAAARRRRR!" Camo and Stinky answered, not even half as loud with their might combined.

Growler looked over his left shoulder and hit the accelerator. The truck peeled down the sidewalk, back in the direction of Marco's house.

"Left!" Growler shouted and turned left toward the road. "Curb!" he announced and veered right to ride two wheels on the curb and two on the road.

When the curb dipped for a driveway, the truck bounced onto all fours. Growler picked up speed before shifting the truck to face the next rise head on. "Air!" he shouted as the curb's rise launched his truck airborne. He waved one arm like a cowboy riding a bucking bronco.

Growler's announcing his moves. Impressive. He wants to race. Marco put two fingers in his mouth and whistled the loudest he could for encouragement.

Growler landed, looked over his shoulder, and then did something that truly put him in the lead for chosen driver. He targeted a huge concrete tube in a neighbor's yard across the street. It was a construction tube, the kind sometimes used in playgrounds for kids to sit in. Growler approached it at an angle. Once he entered it, he turned hard up the slope. Loop-the-loop-the-loop-the-loop until he flew out the other side, rotating, and bounded, luckily, back onto his wheels. He spun to a stop and revved. His tentacles shot straight out and quivered.

Rrrrooooaaaarrrrr! The truck trilled.

"RRRROOOOAAAARRRRR!" Growler boomed.

"RRRROOOOAAAARRRRR!" everyone answered. When he reached Growler, Marco scooped him up and lifted him high.

"Monsters can drive!" he shouted, elated.

All anyone listening would have heard was, "RRRROOOOAAAARRRRR!"

Chapter 23

Whispers

Word of the race spread through school like germs in play-dough. Marco underestimated how much people talk over the weekend, how exciting a dare is, and how much a race could break the monotony of a school-just-started weekend.

The way Marco saw it, September weekends could be great or awful. They were great for older kids in fall sports whose parents showed up to watch and celebrate. Those families usually spent all of their Saturdays together, at fútbol or football or lacrosse or hockey.

But September weekends could be awful for younger kids *not* in organized sports because they didn't have much to do. Even worse, the weather was still summery but the adults in their lives were totally *done* with outside fun. It didn't matter if it was warm enough to kayak the lake, the answer was *there'll be no kayaking.* Or if the days were dry enough to bike the nature path, it was *no biking for buttercup.* Or if the air turned crisp and the leaves were falling, it was *nope, no walking, quit asking, and don't you have chores to do?* Sometimes, grownups dead tired of sweating all summer *might* offer a compromise, but it usually wasn't a good one. Like a long, boring drive through a state park. The first 10 minutes might be cool, but a full hour looking out the window seeing leaves blur by? *Blech.* They were better off waiting until mid-October, just ahead of Halloween, to check back in with the then-rested adults.

So, it turned out that a lot of Marco's friends would have zilch-nada to do in a week's time and were absolutely dying to see who'd win a truck race between a monster and a robot.

By lunchtime, Rosita and Maite were talking about the logistics of crowd control. They, along with Tinker and Knox, sat at Marco's table because race details were something they had to chew through together and Marco wasn't foolish enough to deny his monsters lunch.

"The whole school might show up," Rosita said, pulling her ponytails upward like rabbit-ear TV-antennas. She played with her hair a lot, Marco noticed, when she was nervous or excited. "Kids from other schools might show up too, and they'll *aaaaall* want to see the race. How can they do that, Maite? How can we keep things from getting wobbly?"

Wobbly was what Rosita called anything that wasn't totally under control. Marco guessed she once heard the word "steady" or "even-keeled" or something, and the opposite to both those words, to her, was wobbly.

"Don't worry, Rosita," Maite said. "I'll set up the course so they can't get in the way or mess things up."

Maite never plays with her hair, Marco noticed. *Actually, she just never seems nervous. Or maybe she can hide it better than most.* He felt nervous just looking at her. Her hair shone.

"Where's the course going to be?" Knox asked casually.

Maite's head whipped his way, swishing that shiny hair with it. "Why do you want to know?"

"I mean, where should I expect to be, to help keep people off the course?"

"Is that why you're interested?"

Knox shrugged and looked toward Tinker, who seemed to change the subject.

"You made it sound like you'd do a lot to create a course," Tinker said. "Maybe you shouldn't also worry about crowds."

"Well, people are planning on watching," Rosita said, now directing her ponytails down, pulling at their tips like bike handles. As the ponytails went down, so did the blue bands corralling them. "Promise ya,' they'll want to be up close."

"Well, don't worry about crowds, anyway," Tinker said and leaned toward Knox to tell him something that only the two of them could hear.

Are they becoming buds now? Marco didn't like their sudden chumminess. *If Knox is planning this with Maite but sharing secrets with Tinker, how fair can this race be?*

Tinker pulled away from Knox and smiled to himself.

Marco tried to stare at Knox the way Knox sometimes did to him, laser focused like he was trying to remember Marco's face, for posterity, before pummeling and rearranging it, but Knox wasn't paying attention and Marco was pretty sure he couldn't pull it off anyway. He wouldn't push the issue. *Tinker can have whatever advantage comes his way. My monsters can beat any of his old robots any day of the week.*

He knew it.

He felt it.

He ... sure hoped so.

Chapter 24

Practice

Marco and his monsters practiced driving every day after school. It was a great way for Camo, Growler, and Stinky to release their pent up energy after a day of sneaking around the building. They moved in the vents quickly and quietly and showed up for a lot of Marco's classes. But they also played in other rooms, he learned, like Señor Ortiz's supply closet, where they found a fake eye on a stand. It was plastic, bigger than a person's eye, and featured a cutaway part to show inner eye anatomy. His monsters like carrying it around and pretending it could see into the future. It apparently told them they'd get extra big desserts every day until the race.

They also like the xylophone Ms. Mira kept on her desk. Camo told him Mr. Sanders, the janitor, opened the door when they were inside, but they managed to hide before he saw them. Marco heard from kids who heard from Mr. Sanders's 8th grade son Cole that his dad convinced Sra. Álvaro he was joking about monsters. He apparently wanted to save his vacation time until later in the school year. So when he didn't see anyone in Ms. Mira's room, he backed out. That's when Marco's monsters decided to play a prank. As soon as he shut the door, they slammed their rubber mallets onto the xylophone. The janitor jumped and ran away screaming.

Growler later heard him tell another grown up that the monsters were back.

"And the principal promised him an even longer vacation," Camo said.

For the whole week, every day after school, Marco and his monsters practiced racing in the attic, in his backyard, and at the playground by the nearby woods. All of the monsters drove, not just because it was fun, but to give Growler a break, and in case Growler couldn't or didn't want to drive on race day, or in case they needed to take over driving for any reason.

Plus, having them all drive gave Marco hilarious video, like the clip of Stinky panicking and screaming and driving in Figure 8s to dodge a dive-bombing blackbird. Watching the attack from Stinky's vantage point was gut-splitting. Growler and Camo screamed with laughter and for days pointed to the sky and shouted, "Blackbird!" just to see Stinky dive for cover. Even Stinky laughed. He knew he was a star, his video the funniest by far.

Another clip showed a sprinkler going off right as Camo drove over it. The spray catapulted the truck's back end, flipping the whole thing. But Camo landed like she'd planned it. An epic save.

Marco had his fun, too. Even though he had to keep the fake controller in his left hand in case adults were watching, he brought his right hand to his mouth to whistle encouragement as loudly and high pitched as he could. He let 'em rip, pushing his lungs until the blasts were ear-splitting. He was surprised the neighbors didn't complain. But it felt great to test his volume. His whistles became his version of a roar, and he felt mighty.

The week flew by in a flash, and, before he knew it, it was Saturday morning.

Race day.

Chapter 25

The Course

Marco couldn't believe how vulnerable he felt sitting in his wagon, blindfolded, with one arm wrapped tight around a backpack of monsters and the other gripping his remote control truck, struggling to keep everything from spilling onto the sidewalk. Rosita pulled the wagon, and Marco was trusting her to take them to the right place, the mysterious race course that she and Maite had somehow managed to keep secret for over a week.

"I love how you decorated your monster truck," Rosita said.

"Thanks, Rosi," he answered. "I painted it."

"Figured. You're good at painting."

Rosita's always got something nice to say. Marco smiled but couldn't tell through the blindfold if Rosita saw him.

"Want me to walk instead?" he asked, worried she'd tire herself out.

"Nope, thanks. I got this."

So Marco sat there feeling heavy and foolish. The last time he felt that foolish was when he sent off the order form for his mail-order monsters, back when he needed new friends but didn't know whether they'd be real. Back then, he was putting a whole lot of hope into a decades-old ad. And now look how things were going.

Rosita showed up at his house at seven in the morning—ridiculously early for a Saturday—with a huge grin on her face and waving a scarf, probably her mom's. It smelled like rose perfume. And it matched Rosita's entire outfit that day—pink jeans, a pink top with a purple cat wearing a yellow glitter bow on one ear, pink sneakers with glitter rainbows, and a pink baseball cap with a unicorn-horn patch on it—the cutest outfit he'd ever seen.

"Remind me why I'm blindfolded?" he asked.

"So you can't help your monsters before you get there."

"Like how?"

"I don't know. That's just what Maite said."

Marco loved that Rosita trusted her sister. And despite how Knox was treating him lately, Marco liked that the Cariños were such a close family. He wondered if Knox was pulling Tinker to the course the same way Rosita was pulling him. Maite would be at the course already.

What did she do to make a race course? Where did she set up? Marco was dying to know.

Stinky snuffled. "You smell nervous," he whispered, to whom, Marco didn't know. Both he and Growler answered, "I'm fine."

Is Growler fine? Marco wondered. A thought he'd been trying to push down crept back up again, that maybe it wasn't fair for his monsters to take this on. Maybe it's not right they fight his battles. *I got them to have friends, but now they're not racing for* fun. *They're racing for my honor. But don't friends defend each other?* It was all very confusing. His mind was clouded with worry, his thoughts as dark as his vision behind the blindfold, and the path as unclear as wherever Rosita was taking them. Marco felt like there was some kind of metaphor there, how the future is muddled and shrouded and you can't know for sure what's right until choices are long past. He knew that he too wouldn't have any answers until he got to the end.

"Growler, remember your training, have confidence in how much you've practiced, and follow your gut, okay?" Marco said. His guilt formed a thick lump in his throat and made it tough to swallow. "Don't take any risks out there. It's just a race. No matter how many people are there or how they react, it's just a race."

It was a bumpy ride, the wheels *tha-thumping* at every sidewalk crack and gaining speed down street ramps. The sun blazed and beat his back. Marco realized they couldn't be going far if Rosita was pulling them. He was imagining the options when Rosita called out, "We're here!"

"Can I take off the blindfold?" Marco asked, not wanting to break race rules.

"Yep!"

He yanked it off. "Old Man Jenkins's junkyard? Of course!" *It's the perfect place. And it explains why Maite set the race time so early, to finish before Old Man Jenkins opens for business. Wait, does Jenkins know we're here?* Then he remembered that Jenkins had given the neighborhood kids permission to go to the field in the back lot if they ever needed a quiet, safe place to 'collect' themselves, as he liked to say it. Jenkins almost never went back there.

The back lot was way, way back. There, the oldest and least valuable junk squatted in low piles and became overgrown with grass. A dozen classic cars with huge bumpers and curvy lines lay rusting. Their decaying parts were out of favor and out of demand. Everything else there was decades old and truly the junk of all junk. Jenkins once told them he was lucky to get two customers a year to that section of the yard, so he let the kids use it and the field if they ever needed a place to escape to, to get away from their daily troubles. He always recommended the library as the best safe place, but "the library ain't always open, which sure is a shame."

Still, Marco could see why they were meeting this early. It was probably best to be done and gone before business officially opened, just in case this was one of those rare days that a customer might want the corroded grille of a 1950s Pontiac Chieftain Catalina. The fact that he could name any car prompted a chuckle. *That's Tinker in my head. That's his influence.*

Marco was relieved Maite hadn't set the course in the main junk yard. That place was dangerous. The junk was piled high. And as customers grabbed what they needed, they re-piled stuff badly, if at all. So the piles were not only high. They were unstable. Plus, the dirt walkways curved and snaked instead of queuing in a neat grid. So if Jenkins said "Go up Column 1 and take a right at Row A," that didn't mean they wouldn't get lost. The layout probably even changed over the years as junk piles grew or shrunk.

"You'll have to get out of the wagon," Rosita said, pointing to a hole in the wooden fence along the side of the property, a block away from the front sidewalk. Old Man Jenkins's dog made that hole two years ago, Marco remembered, chasing a thief off the property. The thief scrambled over the fence. The dog ran through it. Marco and Tinker saw it with their own eyes. Jenkins eventually decided rats were a bigger threat than thieves, so when the dog passed away, he rescued two cats from a barn program to be his new mousers. And, boy howdy, were those cats mean. *Would they be locked up?*

Rosita stored the wagon in the bushes across from the hole while Marco secured his backpack and tucked the truck under his arm. Once inside the fence line, Marco stopped, shocked. Half the school was there, and he assumed the other half wasn't there *yet* because it was so early. A bunch of kids he didn't recognize. *Maybe from other schools?*

"Maite texted Jimena this morning with the race place. And then she did her thing."

News outlets would drool, Marco thought, *to have the kind of reach Jimena has.*

When the kids noticed Marco, they silenced.

Yikes. Unnerving. But I asked for this, didn't I, a chance to show off my monsters and one-up Tink? Still, imagining *something and actually living it are two different things.* He knew he had to ignore the pressure. He looked around to get a lay of the land.

One of the first things he noticed was a row of TV monitors atop a long pile of junk on the far side of a dirt walkway. That pile wasn't there before. On the nearer side of the walkway was a folding table supporting three computers. The setup looked like the command deck of a shoddy spaceship. And who was the captain? None other than Tinker.

"Don't worry, he didn't know ahead of time where the race was gonna be," Rosita said. "Knox must've just now helped him bring in all this stuff."

"Why?"

Rosita tilted her head at him. "To be helpful."

"No," Marco said with a little laugh. "I mean, why even have all this stuff?"

"So people can see the race without being tempted to get on the track," Maite said, walking toward him. She wore a flowered top and jeans, both so smeared in mud and dust that he couldn't be certain of the color. "Remember when Tink told us not to worry about crowds? This is why. He had a plan." She stepped up to him, and Marco had the distinct feeling she was resisting the urge to jab his chest with her finger. "Tink knew people on the track could get in the way of the racers, maybe cause them to crash and hurt themselves or others. Tink specifically said he didn't want the monsters to get hurt. And you know what he said when I asked about his robots? He said robots could be repaired."

Marco didn't know how to respond, so he looked toward Tinker and found him walking his way. Tinker was wearing a brown leather utility belt, loaded with screwdrivers, cables, and electric tape, over his grey T-shirt and black jeans. He looked like he owned the place.

"Marco," Tinker said, meeting his eye before looking at a tiny piece of electronics in his hand small enough to be a walkie-talkie for a mouse. He also had a spare helmet cam.

"Antwone," Marco answered flatly.

Tinker ignored the use of his given name. "If you let me put this transmitter on your monster's helmet cam, like I did for my robot, that receiver"—he pointed to a black box taped halfway up a light pole—"can display its video on the monitors. The crowd'll be able to see first-person action without having to run behind the trucks or get in the way."

Marco blinked at him. "Soooo, the crowd can see the action, like in a pro race?"

"Yeah. That all right?"

Marco was awestruck at Tink's skills. He nodded and swung his backpack off his shoulder. His monsters stepped out. Growler, his helmet crooked under his elbow, took an extra step forward.

Rosita hopped from one foot to another and started singing. *She's really amped.*

Tinker bent down and said something to Growler that Marco didn't hear. But Growler nodded, so it must have been okay. Tinker gently took Growler's helmet, attached the thingee he'd made to Growler's cam, and walked back to his command deck. He flicked a switch and *voilà!* Views from two helmets flickered onto two screens above. Growler's cam showed Rosita's dancing feet. The robot's cam—*did the robot have a name?*—showed the inside of an open box. Four other scenes, high views of the track, played out across the other monitors.

"Knox just set those up," Maite said, pointing to various tall structures: the boom of a construction backhoe; a wooden windmill; an old-fashioned clothes rack; and a pyramid of cracked neon signs. "He taped cameras onto all of them." She looked sheepish. "I was surprised he climbed that high after our bet this summer."

Marco distinctly remembered the bet as the moment he started falling for Maite. Then he thought of Knox and how he was actually *helping* with this race. "Oh," he answered. It wasn't enough to say about either Knox or Tinker, but Marco felt that those few good acts couldn't make up for loads of bad ones. Still, he turned to Tinker. "I could have come early to help set up, if I'd have known. I mean, the race is both our responsibilities."

Tinker looked down and took a moment before saying, "Well, I didn't think you'd want to be around me or whatever. I mean—we just— anyway, I haven't seen the track layout."

O-kay. At least the race is still fair.

Rosita paused her bouncing. "This is really cool, what you did, Tink." She started moving again, this time rocking side to side. She kept looking around too. Marco had never seen her so excited. She apparently couldn't stand it any longer because she threw her arms around her sister and asked, "Is it time, MaiMai?"

Maite enveloped her in dusty arms and answered, "Sí, Chaparrita." *She called her Shorty! Sweet.* "Why don't you tell people we'll be starting in a minute? I'll let you know what comes next." Rosita ran off, pumped by her new responsibility. Maite turned back to Marco and Tinker.

"Well? Are you two knuckleheads sure you want to do this? I mean, yeah, people are here, but so what? You two could just apologize and be done with it."

Chapter 26

On your mark...

Marco felt the blood draw from his face. He wasn't sure about much of anything anymore. It was true, a few weeks ago, he'd forgotten to meet Tinker at the junkyard, and that triggered their fight. But Tinker could have been a lot less mean about it. *And it was the first day of school. I had stuff on my mind.* But Marco couldn't back down now. Growler had trained for this race—for a whole week. *He wants to race. And Stinky and Camo have been looking forward to it too. I can't let them down. But they think it's just for fun, and that's...totalmente falso, not at all true. And Tink's spent a lot of time preparing his robot. Seguro que sí, for sure. I mean, if that robot really can drive, shouldn't Tink have a chance to show it off? But can't we do that another time? And what if Tinker wins?*

Marco didn't want to think about that. He'd never live it down. Neither would Tinker. They couldn't stop the race now, could they? *But what would the race prove, anyway?*

"No answer? I guess you still want to race," Maite said. She raised her hands like, why-do-I-put-up-with-them, and dropped them to slap her thighs. Dust puffed loose.

She bent down to Growler, who was twisting his torso side to side and swinging his arms like a batter at home plate, ready for action. Tinker ran back to his computers, pulled something from underneath the table, and returned. It was his robot. It looked like a tin action figure, silvery and jointy. It was a bit smaller than Growler and had a big, blue, power pack in the middle of its chest. Tinker set it down, where it didn't move.

"You'll start there," Maite told the racers, pointing to a line of white, powdered chalk cutting across the dirt pathway. "You'll do three laps." She held up three fingers. "Follow the path marked with signs that are yellow-and-black-striped. Growler?" She looked directly at him. "This is what they look like." She pulled a striped card out of her back pocket. "Follow these stripes until you pass this spot three times, not including the start. If you lose track or can't count, don't worry. You'll hear a siren at the beginning of the final lap. Understand?"

Growler thumped his chest and nodded.

She looked up at Tinker. "Can you set Clank to follow these stripes?"

Clank?! That's awesome. Marco wished he'd have helped come up with that name.

"I thought stripes would be easier for him to spot than a solid color," Maite continued. "Solid colors are everywhere."

"Good call," Tinker answered, "and yes." He pulled his phone from his utility belt and started typing, probably texting directions. Clank's head swiveled as it sought Maite's card. Marco heard a *zzzzzztttt*, like it had zoomed its camera eye onto the target. When Clank had apparently catalogued the stripes in his motherboard or whatever, Tinker holstered his phone.

Now that the racers were side by side, Growler raised his palm for a high five. Clank just looked at it until Tinker again pulled his phone and programmed Clank to tap Growler's hand. When the robot finished, it just sort of ... turned and spaced out.

Awkward, Marco thought. *I wonder if his driving will be as clunky as his social skills?*

"This won't be a straight race," Maite warned the two tiny competitors, as if the robot could hear. *Could it hear?* "Expect impediments." When Growler tilted his head, she clarified, "Snags, hurdles, trouble." He straighted his head, and she nodded, signaling it was time to start. "May the outcome settle this ridiculous score."

She flipped a coin to determine starting positions, then headed toward the track. Growler and Clank followed. The robot seemed more awake now, even looking around. Marco and Tinker scooped up their trucks and followed the racers, who waved like celebrities at the chattering crowd. Kids sat at the edge of the track, not wanting to miss a thing.

Maite set the race to go clockwise, opposite pro racing. Marco set his truck a few feet behind the starting line, on the inner part of the track, away from the kids. Tinker set his the same distance back, but on the outer part of the track, closer to the kids. Marco looked down the course for obstacles, but couldn't see any. *Maite must've set them up after the first curve. More of a surprise that way*, he guessed. Marco and Tinker walked back to the console area, where Tinker would control the video feed. Marco *totally* wasn't going to talk to him, he decided. He just wanted to be close, in case Tinker had something to say.

Camo and Stinky scrambled up Marco's side to the top of his head. They grabbed his hair to hold on. Marco felt a crowd pushing in. When he looked down, Stinky and Camo wobbled atop his crown. A bunch of small kids were reaching up toward them.

"Hey! Don't you know not to touch someone without their permission?" Marco barked, angry he had to again defend his monsters' space. "Don't get grabby."

"My parents don't believe monsters exist," Clarita said. "I'm beginning to think so too."

Marco frowned. His class line-leader had seen the monsters before. She screamed the first day he'd taken them to school when they roared their way out of his backpack. She almost tattled on him when they'd escaped into the ductwork. She had even seen him feed them. *Why is she doubting her own eyes? Why is she dissing them right before the race? Infuriating.*

Clarita put her hands on her hips. "Are these trained monkeys in costume?"

"Clari, do you think I could teach monkeys to talk and do all the stuff these guys do?"

Clari crossed her arms, apparently unconvinced, but Marco didn't care. He looked to the starting line and found Growler tightening his helmet's shoelace strap. Growler gave him a wave, hopped on his truck, and advanced to the starting line. Tinker's robot did the same. The crowd of grabby kids broke away and sat with the others at the edge of the track. A few began chanting.

*"A monster and a robot,
Race around the yard.
Just one crash,
They'll end up charred."*

"Hey! Cut that out!" Maite shouted. "I'll throw out the very next one of you I hear say that. ¡Sinvergüenzas!"

A few of those "shameless" kids chuckled and brought their phones out. Marco could see they were live streaming. He had a dream of just that the night before—big crowds, viral videos, and alerts to the authorities about monster-robot invasions. In his dream, the FBI swooped in to investigate. *But if Clari can't believe Growler is real and she stood right next to him, how could the internet believe it? What exactly do I have to worry about?*

His thoughts were interrupted by Maite addressing the crowd. She gave an introduction to the race. She pointed to the screens to discourage anyone from getting near the course, and all the phones turned to show the monitors. Then—Marco swallowed hard—Maite raised a green scarf—also probably her mom's—and said, "Racers, on your mark."

Marco hadn't had a final chance to give Growler a really good, rousing, fiery pep talk. And there he and Clank were, sitting atop their trucks and gripping the controls.

"Get set!" Maite rose to her tiptoes to lift the scarf higher.

Marco also wanted to tell Growler to be careful and to not get hurt and to watch out for himself and, finally, to have fun.

Maite swept the scarf downward, and shouted, startling Marco and making Camo and Stinky pull his hair in excitement or worry, he couldn't tell which.

"GO!"

Chapter 27

Lap One

The trucks' wheels spun, churning dirt, and everyone watched—in real life and through their phone—as the trucks took off. Marco couldn't believe how fast they were. He hadn't modified his truck, and he knew Tinker's truck was back to spec. That was part of the bet. *And Tink's as good as his word.* Marco's eyes darted from the racers peeling down the straightaway to the monitors. Seeing the race in POV—point of view—helmet cams, was completamente chévere, 100 percent awesome. Plus, the other cameras around the track showed high-angle views. The broadcast was both too much and absolutely perfect.

"Wow! Look at 'em go!" Rosita called. She had a fat silver microphone in one hand and swept her other hand toward the monitors.

"Rosita's calling the race?" Marco called to Maite over the thundering cheers.

She nodded. "And Knox is track tech. He'll change the course each lap and clean it up if it gets messy."

Uh oh. Marco was suddenly extremely worried about the fairness of this race. Knox had gotten awfully chummy lately with Tinker. It would be easy for Knox to make the race harder on Growler. *Would he do that?*

"Growler and Clank are side by side going into the first turn," Rosita announced.

Marco looked to the monitors and saw what the racers couldn't. Coming up was a tight right turn into the first obstacle. *What was that first obstacle, exactly?* It glinted in the sun, so he couldn't tell. Not that he could warn Growler anyway. He had no way to communicate with him. But, he realized, Tinker might be able to command his robot. *Text him, maybe. Use some kind of radio. Morse code. Light waves. Is that sci-fi stuff?* Marco didn't know. It didn't matter. Marco just wished he could help Growler more.

The crowd's noise was deafening. The racers sped into the first turn and started to slide.

"Oh, no! They're going into the turn too fast. They're skidding out!" Rosita called.

Marco watched as Clank's truck slid toward some yoga mats propped on their side. *Ha! What great turn pads.* The mats looked newish, not like they came from the junkyard. *Did Maite take those from her mom?*

As Marco watched, Growler, on the inside, tipped up onto two wheels.

"This is bad for Clank," Rosita called, "and worse for Growler. Either could crash out."

Marco frowned at her, but she wasn't looking his way. He was glad for that. He rearranged his face. *It's not her fault. She's telling the truth.* It just annoyed him that Tinker's robot could actually self-drive. Like, wasn't that some sort of technological breakthrough?

"¡Wepa! Whoo hoo! They slide, they bump, they nearly topple, but they're back on all fours and heading to the first obstacle!"

Marco saw it all and had to admit it was glorious seeing the race this way. Through their helmet cams, just a foot above ground. Dirt below, junk around and above. Yellow-and-black cards tacked around the track and metal glinting up ahead. Plus, Rosita's play-by-play was awesome. He looked to Maite.

"Toda la semana, viendo videos," Maite explained. "She's been practicing all week, watching car races and speedskating on YouTube, repeating everything the announcers say. She's really learned the lingo."

"Como un campeona," Marco agreed. *Like a total champ.*

The crowd noise surged as Clank zipped ahead of Growler. Marco shifted his eyes to another monitor and caught sight of the obstacle before a glint of sunlight obscured it once more. *Hubcaps.* They were laid out on the course like cones. No way to avoid them.

Clank swerved left to set up his entry between the first two hubcaps. Growler swerved right. The crowd gasped, now able to see for themselves the trouble that lay ahead. Clank led by only a truck-length. Would they collide when they both swerved in?

"Swivel, swivel, swivel, swivel!" shouted Camo and Stinky. Growler had done this before. *Would he remember?* Marco held his breath as he watched the monitors.

Clank left.

Growler right.

Swerve, swerve, swerve, swerve. Criss cross. Criss cross. Exiting out the other side, they came within inches of each other. Marco let out a raspy breath. No crash and no one charred, unlike the kids' cruel song.

Clank steered toward the outer edge of the track for the next turn.

"Go wide!" Stinky shouted, as if Growler could hear him. Didn't matter, though, 'cause Growler did it on his own. He positioned himself behind Clank to draft off the leader.

Drafting, Marco remembered, was another thing Tinker had taught him. "A racer suffers less air drag if he settles in behind someone so that other racer gets hit with the brunt of the atmospheric pressure." Growler could ride easy in Clank's wake and even get a fraction of a second more reaction time after the turn.

It was beautiful watching on helmet and high-angle cameras as the trucks entered the turn wide, cut in at the curve's apex, and swung out wide again. Only, with Growler drafting, he had more speed. He whooshed past Clank to the roar of the crowd.

"A pass! Growler passes to take the lead!" screamed Rosita.

"YAAAAAAY!" shouted Stinky and Camo, both nearly ripping out Marco's hair. Marco shouted too, along with everyone else. If Rosita said anything else about the pass, no one heard.

"The next obstacle," called Rosita.

Marco saw in a high-angle monitor two large black splotches on either side of the track. The crowd yelled in unison, "Oil!"

Both drivers could've whizzed between the oil spills if they'd been center track, but they were going full speed and weren't lined up. *FSHZZZZ!* The trucks drove through. Oil sprayed everywhere, covering the racers and track. They lost traction and began to spin.

"Growler!" Marco watched in horror. The crowd hooted in delight. The trucks collided, broke the spin, and ended facing forward as before, having barely lost any speed.

"Clank and Growler regain control," Rosita reassured the crowd.

Me muero, Marco thought. This race was gonna kill him. He looked to Tinker, who looked almost sick. *Is he really that worried for Growler?* He watched Tinker move a little stick on the command console to tilt a camera farther down the track.

Growler still led by half a truck-length as the drivers brought their trucks back to speed. Marco could see by Clank's helmet cam that Growler was smiling and talking with him and pumping his fist like he was having the time of his life. Clank, of course, wasn't making any moves like that, *but could he understand?* Marco wondered. *Could he talk? Was he encouraging Growler like Growler was encouraging him? Probably not because that'd make him, like, almost* alive. *But he wasn't alive, not like Growler was.* Marco suddenly felt sorry for Tinker. *Tink's friends aren't real. They're machines. They can't feel or care, not like real friends. At least not yet. That tech doesn't exist yet, not even in Tink's lab.*

"They're having fun out there. At least Growler is," Rosita announced. "And here comes another obstacle, their first big challenge!"

Heads and phones turned like a wave toward the most-right monitor.

"Go! Go! Go!" chanted Camo and Stinky. The crowd leapt to its feet.

The racers' helmet cams showed it best, their trucks bouncing on the dirt path and quickly approaching a long, wooden plank which led into the driver's side of a weatherbeaten old car. The car door was one of those rare ones that opened backward, and Marco instantly knew it wasn't just *any* old car. It was a bent and beaten—but still spectacular—fire-engine-red 1937 Talbot Lago coupé, nicknamed The Teardrop because it was nothing but curves. Marco realized, yet again, that he only knew that because of Tink. So he knew that car was made in France. Its steering wheel was on the right side of the car, opposite where Growler would enter.

Growler bounded full speed onto the plank. *Oof,* his helmet cam shook when he hit it. And then he was racing up the steep incline. When he reached the top, his truck pushed a metallic red flag that swung back at contact. It triggered an old-fashioned car horn.

AHWOOOOGA!

Everyone laughed. Marco saw Growler's fist pump and heard a faint roar. *He loves it.*

Growler's truck bounced across the mostly intact bench seat of The Teardrop. Marco had seen bench seats before, on his various treks to the yard with Tinker. They were like one long sofa that stretched across the car. Marco couldn't imagine how much more comfortable it must have been to sit on that than always being strapped in to bucket seats. He laughed, watching Growler's POV bounce across the seat as if he were in a moon castle.

Another *AHWOOOOGA*! and everyone knew Clank had hit the turnstile.

Back to Growler's view, Marco saw him reach out and slide a hand across the car's steering wheel. He rode the next wooden plank down to the dirt track.

Ha! Marco was super glad Growler could experience such a fun ride.

Both racers next faced two right turns. Clank cut on the inside to catch up. *Smart.* When they entered the opening straightaway, they were neck and neck. Growler was shouting and smiling at Clank, holding a whole conversation, apparently.

If that doesn't convince the internet that Growler is real, nothing will. A few kids lowered their phones, Marco guessed, to check viewer comments.

As the racers passed the crowd, Growler furiously waved to them.

Rosita looked pleased as poppies to call, "On to Lap Two!"

Chapter 28

Lap Two

Marco saw on the high-angle cams that someone—*Knox, obviously, since Maite put him in charge of the track*—had moved the yoga mats for Lap Two. The turn wasn't as tight. Marco sighed in relief.

The racers drove side by side and handled the new turn better. Clank was on the inside, so his path was shorter. He took the lead as they bore down on two plastic pipes, each about two feet wide, much smaller than the concrete pipe Growler had used for loop-the-loops. The pipes' openings were draped with mop heads—dirty and ropey. They looked a lot like the mane on the horse in Marco's. Clank drove in, sending the ropes flapping and disappearing into the pipe.

Growler's truck reeled as he spun to a hard stop.

"Oh no!" Rosita shouted into the microphone. "Growler's stopped. Something's wrong."

Everyone looked to the monitors, trying to figure out the problem.

"He scared!" Stinky shouted, prompting a few kids to look his way.

Marco felt weight on his head shift and soon heard Camo whisper, "Even monsters sometimes need help to be brave."

Marco didn't know what he was supposed to do. The rules he and Tinker had decided on said they couldn't go onto the track once the race started unless there was a true emergency. This wasn't one. *Help to be brave?* He could only think of what had already worked before, when his biggest monster showed feats of strength. Marco started chanting, "Growl-er! Growl-er!"

He felt movement overhead and heard Camo and Stinky join in. "Growl-er! Growl-er!"

Soon others added their voices. Rosita thrust the mic toward the crowd so their encouragement could maybe, hopefully, be heard on the track. Motion drew Marco's eyes, and he caught Tinker doing did the most amazing thing. His ex-bestie reached for the volume slider on his sound board and pushed it all the way up. Speakers around the track crackled as the crowd's chant reverberated through the yard.

"Growl-er! Growl-er! Growl-er! Growl-er!"

Marco stopped chanting even though Camo and Stinky and everyone else were still at it. He stood transfixed, staring at Tinker. *Why did he do that? Why didn't he let Growler be out there all scared and alone?*

The chant morphed into a cheer. Marco turned from Tinker to the monitors to see Growler looking up. *He can hear the chants.* The fierce, red, gorilla-looking monster threw his arms wide, as if soaking up the sun, then crashed one fist, then the other, onto his chest.

Thump. Thump. Thump, thump, thump, thump, thump.

Marco pumped his arm into the air just as Growler slammed his down onto the truck.

Rrrrooooaaaarrrrr! The truck trilled.

"RRRROOOOAAAARRRRR!" Growler boomed.

"RRRROOOOAAAARRRRR!" The crowd howled.

"RRRROOOOAAAARRRRR!" screamed Marco, Camo, and Stinky.

Growler spun the truck to face his fear. He thrust the thumbstick forward for power and shot toward the mop head. Everyone cheered, including Clarita, Marco noticed. But when he looked back to

Tinker, he found him typing on his phone, distracted.

Marco went back to Growler's POV. Growler plowed through the mop head, into the long, dark pipe. A growing circle of light ahead showed not much more to go. Growler was going full tilt. He wanted outta there asap—and maybe wanted to catch up to his new friend, Clank.

Leave it to monsters to make friends with an enemy, Marco thought before correcting himself. *But Tinker isn't an enemy, Neither is Clank. They're just ... temporary competitors.* Marco liked that choice of phrase. *Temporary* felt better than *permanent,* and they *were* just competitors. The truth was, he realized, he wasn't burning-hot mad anymore. He was beginning to think the whole thing was foolish, what they'd fought over.

"Look at this," someone—*maybe a fourth-grader?*—said, showing off his phone. "My video has ten thousand views already." Marco didn't have time to care. He watched Growler shoot out of the tube, Clank nowhere to be seen. Growler hit the next turn too fast, tipped, and drove high skis—on his two back wheels—before shifting to drop the truck back to earth.

Secure in the straightaway, Growler pushed the accelerator—*just to feel wind,* Marco was sure—and in an instant swerved to avoid something in his path. He had just cleared it when his POV cam showed a 180-degree turn as he glanced over his shoulder.

"Clank and his truck are sunk in mud," Rosita announced. "Look at those wheels spin! How is Clank going to escape that pit?"

Growler passed Clank not knowing what he was seeing.

Sure enough, Growler's car skidded to a bumpy stop, which meant he switched to reverse while going full speed. *Impressive.* The next thing he knew, Growler was backing up.

"What's this?" Rosita asked into the microphone. "Looks like Growler's giving up an easy chance to win. He's off his truck."

Everyone watched Growler bound onto the track, bumble over to the mud pit, and wade in. Marco imagined his feet going *schloop schloop* as he sunk in the muck. The sludge reached his knees and coated the truck's wheels.

"Why's your truck sinking like that?" Marco asked Tinker without thinking.

"Clank weighs more than Growler." Tinker forgot too, apparently, that they were giving each other the cold shoulder. "The more features I added, the heavier he got."

Features like incredible navigation? Marco wondered, but he had a bigger question. *Why is there a mud pit deep enough to swallow half a truck? That's dangerous.* His eyes swept the crowd and spotted Maite yelling into her phone. Beside him, Tinker secured an earpiece to his own phone. *Is he answering Maite's call or dealing with his robot?*

Marco wanted answers, but the race was more important. He saw Growler raise his hands to Clank, like *hold on,* and he schlepped farther into the pit. His mouth was moving.

Is... is he reassuring him?

Growler patted Clank's muddy back and plodded to the back of the truck. He waved one arm to signal Clank before squatting low and digging both hands in the mud.

Clank revved. Mud sprayed in two soaring arcs over and onto Growler.

"What's he doing?!"

"Growler's back there!"

Clank's tires churned as they went full power. Mud sprayed Growler's chest, his shoulders, his face. A horrifying thought struck Marco: *Can Growler breathe?* He was about to run out when Stinky climbed down and put a hand on his neck. "Marco waitses," he said.

Growler was nearly buried in the sludge being fire-hosed at him. But he finally straightened his back and lifted the back end of the truck. Clank revved a few times, and Growler caught the rhythm. He pushed the truck with each forward lurch. One, two, three pushes, and the truck surged free, blasting muck across Growler, who fell under the torrent.

"Growler!" Rosita yelled. Her voice sounded so different that Marco swiveled to see. Her microphone hung at her side, forgotten. She had called out directly to Growler.

Marco set a hand on Stinky so they could run onto the track, but this time Camo scrambled down and pulled his ear.

"What?!" Marco bellowed, annoyed they kept stopping him.

"Let me try," Camo said in Growler's voice.

Marco shook his head, disbelieving. *Why don't they want to help?* But it occurred to him that maybe his monsters knew more about each other than he did. Maybe Growler didn't need to breathe as much as people. Maybe Growler would want to prove he could handle problems. *Like I'd want to.* He looked back to the monitors. Clank was free, in the clear. He could win the race, easy. But Growler was buried in mud, his helmet cam showing the darkness of a grave.

Get up, buddy. Seconds ticked by—only a few, Marco knew, but they felt like forever. *Please, Growler, I need to see that you're okay.* And then he realized something solid, something sure. *I don't care about the race, buddy. Just get up.*

"What's Clank doing?" someone asked.

Marco scanned the line of monitors to see Clank running toward the mud pit. As soon as he got in, his pace slowed. The goo was grabby. When Clank got to the big brown lump that was Growler, he maneuvered to stand behind him, dug his hands into the muck, and pulled. His point of view showed a puff of air burst out of the mud, launching strings of slime. The lump grew less muddy as Clank kept pulling it further out of the pit. Finally Clank reached dry ground and collapsed with Growler on top of him.

Marco's stomach dropped back into place. He covered his face with his hands. If he didn't cry, he was going to puke—or cry *and* puke.

"WhoooHOOO!" Rosita cheered. The crowd went wild cheering, bouncing on their butts, scrambling to stand. A few came over to slap Marco and Tinker on the back. Tinker looked sick.

"They're all right," Rosita told the crowd. "And they're both cleaning up in their own way." In the monitors, Growler shook like a dog, sending gobs of mud flying, and Clank squeegeed himself with his robot hands. "Hold on. What are they doing now?"

Growler and Clank returned to their trucks. When Growler settled on top of his, he turned it around and drove it back to the turn. Clank stood beside his truck, watching. At Growler's wave, he mounted his truck and signaled back. Both drivers started again, continuing their race where they'd been before Clank hit the mud pit.

Marco didn't think it was possible, but he suddenly felt even worse. He covered his face again, not out of fear of puking but something else.

"Growler good friend," Stinky whispered in Marco's ear.

Marco lowered his hands to see Tinker staring at him, also not looking great.

"No one believes my video!" whined a voice Marco recognized as Lupita, a girl in his grade he didn't share classes with. She waved her phone. "A commenter asked about Marco and Tinker, and when I said one's an artist and the other is a techie, they called the whole thing fake. And everyone's agreeing!" A few kids lowered their phones in defeat.

Out of the corner of his eye, Marco saw Tink remove his earpiece.

"Who were you talking to?" Marco asked.

"No one. Entirely listening."

That struck him. "Were you ... listening to Growler?" Marco asked.

"Yeah," Tinker said. "When Growler stopped, I was surprised. But I had a feeling he might talk to Clank, and I wanted to help Clank communicate so Growler wouldn't think Clank was mad, if that's what he might think. But I don't really know what Growler might think. I just directed Clank—by text—to do whatever he said."

"That's sorta directing your driver."

Tinker bit his lip. He was caught red handed. Neither was supposed to help their driver. But Marco didn't dwell on the rule-breaking. Instead, he latched onto something different. *If Tink told Clank to obey Growler, Tink was trusting that Growler wouldn't tell his robot to slow down or throw the race. Growler wouldn't, of course, but Tink didn't know that. It's me who knows Growler just wants to make friends.* Following that chain of thought, Marco realized that if he and Tink had been friends during all this, Tink would've known Growler better.

"Your monsters are really cool," Tinker said quickly, as if afraid he'd lose his nerve.

"Clank is too." Marco admitted with a sigh.

"The next obstacle," declared Rosita, "makes the racers go *over* the car, not through like last time, and the climb would be tough for any monster truck!" She thrust her microphone toward the sky.

Marco stared. *How much did she practice to be able to call a race this well?*

Clank reached The Teardrop again, this time ahead of Growler. His helmet cam showed another wooden ramp, this one on its side so it became a short, wide plank leading to the front bumper. Clank would have to pick just the right spot to climb it. Marco looked to Tinker, who lifted his hands off the console, palms out, showing *This is all Clank.*

Rosita grew silent. Marco was enthralled. She clearly knew that silence would build excitement. Or, that saying anything might help the racers beat the challenge. Either way, *way cool.* She pressed her lips together.

Everyone watched as Clank leaned forward to gather speed. Marco and Tinker were familiar with that car, and both knew that what *looked* like the easiest way to climb it was the worst way to go. The Teardrop had five rises: the center one, two over the headlights, and the two outer-most beauties hugging the wheels. The last two were steep but nothing compared to the center rise, so they might *look* like the way to go, but they soon dipped and ended at the big bulge of the back wheels. Nowhere to go but back. The rises over the headlights were less steep, nice and easy, but they led to the same dead end. The only way over that car was by beating its steepest, most intimidating rise, right up the center, over the engine grille and hood. It wasn't *exactly* like hitting a wall, but it was close enough. *Clank's gonna need a lotta speed to beat that.*

Tink looked worried, which confused Marco. *What's the problem? If Clank crashes, he can be fixed.* But as Marco watched, he had another thought, a more generous thought now that he wasn't so mad. *Maybe Tink doesn't want something he put time and care into being destroyed.*

It turned out they didn't need to worry. Clank was a robot who could calculate the odds.

On his approach, Clank centered himself to the plank and leaned so far forward that at any other time he'd have pitched right over the front of the truck. Instead, the added momentum gave him just enough speed to ride the grille to the hood. The flat expanse there provided time to rebuild speed for the windshield. Once on the roof, Clank hit reverse to slow before sliding down the back window, trunk, and plank.

"Expert level!" Rosita shouted. Tinker slapped a hand to his forehead, he was so relieved.

"He did great," Marco told him. Tinker answered with a withered smile.

"Growler's turn!" Rosita called. Marco was surprised to see that Growler wasn't so far behind anymore, maybe because he was lighter than Clank. But being lighter wouldn't help here.

Growler was practically a jet, which was great because his speed compensated for his lighter weight. After pitching forward for the rises and barely making it, he leaned back to slow on the roof so he wouldn't fly clean off the end. He got back on track like a pro and took the final turn to the straightaway.

"Everyone get ready," Rosita called. "Here comes Lap Three!"

Chapter 29

Lap Three

When Clank zoomed past the crowd, the air suddenly filled with the unmistakeable *RAAAAAHHHHHRRRREEEEEE* of an old-timey air-raid siren. *Ha! So that's the sound marking the last lap.* Marco looked around for Maite and found her on the other side of Tink, hand-cranking what looked like a big fishing reel encased in olive-green metal. Maite must have rescued the siren while scoping the race course. It sounded perfect amongst this old junk.

A second siren assaulted his ears. Marco leaned his head away from Camo, on his shoulder, to see her mouth open, imitating the siren perfectly. *RAAAAAHHHHHRRRREEEEEE*. The crowd soon joined in, Rosi loudest of all. Growler waved wildly as he zoomed past.

"He's having the time of his life," Marco said, suddenly sad that he and Tinker weren't doing the same. The moment he thought it, Camo leapt onto Tinker's shoulder.

"Whoa!" Tinker's arms shot out like he was walking a tightrope. Camo didn't say a word but instead camouflaged against Tink to nearly disappear beside his neck. Marco smiled to himself. *That's really cool of her.*

"We're at the opening turn of the third and final lap," Rosita called. "Trust me, folks, this lap will be MEOW-velous."

Marco and Tinker snapped to attention.

Anyone else might have thought she was drawing attention to the cat on her T-shirt or just being cutesy, but Marco and Tinker knew better. They'd visited Old Man Jenkins's Junkyard enough to have scrapes with his two cats, who were friendly only to Jenkins. Otherwise, they were "working cats" with a job to do, and that job wasn't welcoming people into the yard. Jenkins had told Marco and Tinker that vermin could take over a junkyard if something didn't keep them away, and no trap worked as well as a cat, two cats being even better. Marco had seen them chase all sorts of creatures: mice, rats, weasels, birds, rabbits, even squirrels, who can definitely fight back. Without Jenkins around, the cats would absolutely think kids were similar pests to be chased off. *Did Maite know that?*

"Oh, noooooo," Marco said slowly, turning to Tinker. "You don't think they'd ..."

"Impossible."

"Clank finishes the turn as Growler enters it," Rosita called.

Everyone's eyes were glued to the monitors. Knox had moved the yoga-mat-turn-pads to create the widest turn yet. The racers handled it easily. What would be harder was what Marco saw ahead: a cage made of wood and wire, Knox sitting on top.

He kicked the door open. Out raced Murder and Mayhem.

"Evasive action!" Tinker shouted.

He must have hoped the racers could hear him, Marco thought, because, even if he and Tinker raced out onto the track that second, the cats would get to the racers before they could.

Sure enough, the black, orange, and white calico cats sprinted toward the racers. Their legs stretched far in huge strides. They weren't looking to simply approach, sniff, and investigate. Oh no, these sisters were out to tackle and kill.

Kids screamed. From fear or amazement, Marco couldn't tell. But even from their distance, looking up at those monitors, any kid could see the cats' long teeth and sharp claws.

Murder bolted toward Clank like a streak of lightning. She was more white than black, with an orange nose, and was the meaner of the two—or more territorial—or perhaps more fearful for her sister's safety. Marco could give her that. No matter what, she was worse and the one everyone had to look out for. Mayhem was mostly black except for her face, which was split down the middle half black, half orange. She charged toward Growler.

They no doubt saw the trucks and their drivers as prey. Clank was mechanical, so he couldn't be eaten. *But Growler? Is he made of meat like other living things?* Marco didn't know.

It all happened so fast.

Before the cats could tackle them, both racers turned outward, toward the outside of the track. The sisters slipped and skidded between them. But this only bought the racers a second. The cats twisted like they were made of liquid, turned course, and went after them again.

Growler and Clank veered inward and locked arms as they passed each other. With their legs tight around their trucks and their arms clasped tight, the centrifugal force lifted their rides off the ground, just for a second, enough to crack both cats in the face and send them stumbling.

The crowd's cheers were so loud, Marco wondered if a neighbor might call the cops.

Growler and Clank almost biffed it when their trucks landed, but they spun the right way and took off.

Murder and Mayhem twitched from top to tail, skin quivering like a pack of angry bees. They regained their bearings, dropped into a crouch, and bolted yet again after their prey.

"Those cats are out to hurt them!" Rosita called, her surprise plain. "Knox! Catch 'em!"

While Marco appreciated Rosi commanding her brother to catch feral cats, he thought no one in their right mind would go after them without a padded suit and a claw-proof net.

A strike against his shoulder made Marco almost jump out of his skin. Camo reappeared there, so excited, her camouflage was flashing every pattern but Marco's. "Don't go!" she said, apparently reading Marco's thoughts to find a padded suit and a claw-proof net. "Watch."

All monitors showed some aspect of the chase. Clank and Growler approached a turn, but the sister cats would surely outmaneuver them if they didn't do something drastic. Just as Marco thought this, Clank positioned his truck behind Growler's and settled against his back bumper. They were going the same speed, a train of morsels for the cats catching up.

Growler popped up onto the roof of his truck. Now that he wasn't pushing the accelerator, it was up to Clank to keep up their speed. His truck wouldn't be able to do that for long. Growler steadied himself and crouched.

"What is he doing?" Rosita asked right before Growler kicked out against a tower of pink plastic alongside the track. Three plastic lawn flamingos came loose.

"I asked Knox to put a camera on the pole behind those flamingos," Tink said, "but he said the stack was too unstable."

Growler plopped back onto his truck just as the entire tower toppled. Both cats swerved to avoid the falling birds, but there weren't just three or ten or thirty. In a flash, there were too many flamingos to count. It was a *flamboyance* of flamingos, and Marco couldn't believe that he remembered reading that somewhere: a flock of flamingos is called a flamboyance. And that was a *spectacular* name for what was happening.

"Way to go, Growler!" shouted Rosita.

You'd think cats would slide on their butts to change direction and avoid an onslaught of crooked-necked plastic birds with metal spikes for legs bouncing and jumbling all over. But not these two. Maybe the sisters were too bent on a fight. Or they just didn't know what they were getting themselves into. But Murder and Mayhem contorted their bodies, dodged, jumped, and even tumbled with them when they couldn't outmaneuver. The cats avoided most of the birds, but the flamingos did their flamboyant job to slow them down. The hunters lost speed and distance, but, wow, were their feline eyes zeroed in on the racers. They. Were. Furious.

"Knox! Yay! Go, big brother! Whoo hoo!" Rosita called.

There was Knox on another monitor, propping yoga mats at the turn, creating a high bank so the racers could take the turn at speed rather than having to slow and risk cat claws.

There were a lot of flamingos still bouncing, but not enough to be endless. Murder and Mayhem escaped the final stragglers and tore up the track toward the yard invaders.

"Growler and Clank take the turn together," Rosita announced. "They're in the back straightaway heading to their final obstacle."

Well, that's super, Marco thought, *but they aren't clear of cats yet.*

Knox yanked the mats away, but Murder and Mayhem didn't need them. They instead bounded into Knox, ricocheting off his chest, and sending him toppling back over a crate. The cats were suddenly in the back straightaway too.

All four charged ahead full throttle, drivers in the lead and feline pursuers behind. Growler's and Clank's trucks weren't fast enough to outpace the predators. Murder and Mayhem, strings of spit flying off their canine teeth, were gaining.

"Faster, Friends! Faster!" Rosita shouted as the crowd got to its feet and bounced on their toes. "Lose the cats here and you're home free!"

Marco and Tinker looked ahead to the final obstacle: a jump, bigger than any Growler had ever done. Marco wondered if Clank had practiced jumps. He had his answer in seconds.

The pair lowered themselves flat onto their truck for the approach. The ramp, if you could call it that, was an old refrigerator door, egg-white, leaned against another refrigerator, this one peachy with rounded corners, laid on its back. Both were from the 1950s, probably, Marco thought, and were missing handles, making for a smooth run. Beyond to the bottom refrigerator was something the racers definitely couldn't see: a rectangular kiddie pool, positioned the long way, filled to the brim with soapy water. It would take a two-and-a-half-meter jump to clear it.

Marco stuck his fingers in his mouth and whistled so high-pitched that it hurt his own brain. Every kid in the junkyard clasped their hands over their ears. The cats flattened theirs. Was the whistle a violation of the rule against communicating with the racers? Possibly, but Marco wasn't about to let cats named Murder and Mayhem get ahold of either little pal. And Tinker was churning his hands, nodding at him to keep it up, so his race opponent clearly didn't mind.

The sisters hurtled ahead but turned their heads side to side, looking for the source of the sound. *Those tiny movements had to slow them down, right?* Marco hoped so.

He was still whistling when the cats got within swiping distance of the racers. But then Growler and Clank hit the ramp. Their trajectory changed as they rose. Murder and Mayhem put a fraction more weight onto their back legs as they swung forward to pounce.

The cats are going to get their hooks into them and rip them to shreds. Marco's chest felt like it was on fire. He couldn't bear losing Growler—but he hadn't done anything to stop it. *Stinky and Camo told me to let him race, but what do they know? All I did was whistle. I didn't run out there to chase off cats or to save our friends. Am I a bad person? An awful friend?*

Murder and Mayhem raised their claws for the kill. But the trucks were still muddy. And the refrigerator door had soapy water on it from whoever had messily filled the kiddie pool. When those muddy wheels hit the soap, they churned the soapy water and siphoned off mud, giving them excellent traction while making the surface worse for the cats. When Growler shouted to Clank to go wide, they did—and just in time.

Murder and Mayhem landed where the racers had been a second ago, in a spot now slippery with soapy sludge. Their eyes widened as they lost control. The refrigerator door was smooth and extra slimy. Their claws could do nothing on its surface. And the cats had momentum. Their legs slipped out from under them. They slammed onto their butts and flailed, helpless to stop, and watched their prey on either side gain speed, well able to handle the surface.

"Haha!" shouted Rosita.

Everyone watched as the trucks, on the outermost edges of the ramp, took off into the air. Their drivers whooped and hollered and raised their arms like roller coaster riders cresting the first lift. They held the trucks by their legs and turned their faces toward each other, Growler smiling big as the sun.

The raging wet cats slid and collided and clawed right up until at the ramp's slippery edge, but they couldn't grab hold. There was no stopping them. They twisted mid-air, hissing like a cracked fire extinguisher, before splashing into the pool below. Marco heard their screeches all the way at the finish line. Then he heard the *KUH-CHUNK* of both trucks landing, followed by the unmistakable *REEEOOOWs* of a cat fight.

The crowd's shouts were even louder than the cats' spits and hisses.

Redirected aggression. Marco could't help but remember reading about it the day Jenkins got his cats and he spotted them chasing off a customer. *If cats are after something, and something else gets in the way, cats'll sometimes turn on that second something.*

"That was amazing!" Tinker shouted.

"Clank and Growler clear the final obstacle!" Rosita screamed into the mic. "Two right turns and they'll enter the home stretch!"

Kids in the crowd were grabbing the shoulders of taller friends trying to hop up and better see. Bigger siblings lifted their smaller siblings. Others just scooped up whoever to help.

"I don't even care who wins," Tinker said.

Marco was surprised Tink said it first. "I don't either, but it'll be fun to see who does."

With that, they both looked to the final turn. Clank was slightly behind but on the inside track so he had the slight advantage of a shorter distance. Growler was in the lead but on the outside, which meant he had more distance to cover around the curve. As they entered the straightaway, they were side by side, Growler chattering and Clank nodding. *What is Growler saying right now? And does Clank understand or is his programming just making him polite?*

It didn't matter. They were even. Their heads were even. Their tires were even. Their bumpers were even. The crowd was screaming. The cameras were rolling.

They raced across the finish line.

And not even instant replay could say who won.

Chapter 30

Win the Crowd

It didn't matter how many times Clarita replayed the videos. No one could say for sure who crossed that line first. The crowd split into three camps: those who thought Growler had won, those who felt Clank had won, and those who were still busy cheering the racers, who had finally slowed down at the end of the straightaway and turned to slowly drive back. Knox lumbered behind them, pinpricks of blood dotting his muddy, soapy shirt. He looked awful.

Marco realized Knox had done a lot today, even before he saved the racers with that banked turn. *Really. He hustled. The whole thing could have ended awfully without him.* Marco was awestruck to realize he felt grateful.

Growler and Clank rolled back down the track, Growler chattering with Clank and pumping a fist toward the crowd. Clank pumped his fist too, and Marco got the impression that Clank was *copying* Growler. *Does Clank admire him? Does Clank even have enough brainpower to admire someone? Or is that getting into scary robot consciousness?*

Growler and Clank neared the finish line, so Marco and Tinker headed over to greet them. They hoisted their racers off their trucks and onto the tops of their heads so everyone could see. All three factions of the crowd gathered to congratulate them for their excellent driving and surprising sportsmanship. Even Knox clapped. And there was Rosita jumping up and down. Growler waved at the crowd, his smile running ear to ear. Clank couldn't smile, but he waved too. They looked like true friends with not another care in the world.

Marco knew it was time. He lowered Growler to his shoulder and turned to face his ex-bestie. He tried to ignore Maite and Knox and Rosita and Clarita and the whole video-replaying crowd, but they made a huge, unexpected audience for what Marco preferred to be a private moment, one that should've happened a long time ago, no matter who started it.

Marco cleared his throat. "Tink," he said, gearing up.

"Speak up! We can't hear you!" called someone from the back. Marco sighed. *Okay, guess I'm the entertainment* after *the entertainment.*

"Tink," he said, much louder, "I'm sorry."

"See?! Clank won!" someone said.

"Shut up! No, he didn't," answered someone else. A few people leaned toward their neighbor and whispered, but Marco couldn't let what they thought, good or bad, stop him now.

"Tink, I wasn't a good friend when you needed me. And, when you pointed it out, I got madder at you for saying it than at myself for having done it. I should've been there for you, and I wasn't. I'm sorry." Marco meant it, and he felt a wave of relief wash over him for saying it. He wondered how long he felt that way. *Pretty soon after the initial fight? So why didn't I say it?* He had some figuring out to do there.

"I'm sorry too," Tinker said. "I overreacted and didn't want to admit it when you said it, even though it was true."

"Friends?" Marco jutted out a hand.

"Friends," Tinker clasped it.

"¡Puaj! It's about time you two made up," Maite said, planting her hands on her hips.

Knox stepped beside her and nodded his way. Marco couldn't tell exactly what that meant, but Knox didn't look angry.

Camo leapt onto Tinker's shoulder and turned fully yellow, cheerful as the sun.

"All right, everybody," Maite called to the crowd, ignoring Camo's move, as if disappearing and reappearing monsters was a daily thing. "Here are your clean-up assignments."

"Ugh, clean up?!" Clari whined.

"It's a junkyard. What's to clean up?" asked a girl who'd spent the race live streaming.

"We have to take down the race course. This back lot isn't how it was before, and we're going to leave this place looking better than when we got here. For Old Man Jenkins's sake."

That won 'em over. Everybody's folks'd bought from him, and OMJ was pretty cool.

"But what about Murder and Mayhem?" Clari asked. She looked back to the monitors as if she expected to see the cats' noses pressed against them, sniffing out new victims.

"Murder and Mayhem will be hiding, licking off the soap and water," Maite said. "But let's hurry anyway." Marco smiled at how she could get her way *and* make people hurry about it.

Maite spent a few minutes directing her new work crew. "You, you, and you, go dump out the kiddie pool and bring it back here. It's Rosita's." And then, "You four, move the wooden planks from the car and lean them against it. Make sure they're secure and won't fall over."

Maite's directions went on until every obstacle was being dismantled or, in the case of the pink flamingos, re-stacked. That job went to the smallest kids because it involved throwing the flamingos in a heap. "Just toss them in a pile. No climbing allowed," Maite warned, wagging her finger at them like climbing was a no-no. "Make sure you don't leave anyone behind. Buddy up. When everybody's done," she said to the group at large, "go out this way, at the fence hole." She pointed at it and then waved. "Hope y'all had fun."

As everyone left to complete their tasks, Maite turned to face her brother.

"What happened with the mud pit?"

Marco remembered the deep, sucking pit that nearly swallowed Growler. And now it sounded like Knox was in charge of it. *So he was the person Maite called during the race.*

Knox turned to face her. "I accidentally dug it too deep. I could tell when I put in the water. And then I meant to kick some dirt into it to dry it." He ran a hand through his dirty blonde hair. "But then you texted me that I had to hurry with the course because Marco had arrived." He frowned. "That meant finishing the mop tunnels and moving the cat crate. I got distracted."

Maite's features softened. "Oh, I'm sorry, Knox. I guess I did give you a lot to do. But you did do great, Ñeco." She turned to look at Tinker and Marco. "Didn't he?"

"Oh, yeah."

"Great."

"Who's Ñeco?" Tinker dared to ask.

Knox clasped a muddy hand over Maite's mouth.

"Ñeco is Knox." Rosita said as Maite pulled Knox's hand away. "It's his real name. Ñeco is short for Muñeco. But he only likes people to call him Knox because it sounds tougher." She turned to hug Knox, who was grimacing as if the cats had pooped in his shoes. "But he *is* a muñeco, aren't you, ñeco? He's my dollie."

Marco rolled his lips inward. He wasn't going to say a thing. Tink's eyes widened, and Marco knew he had figured it out: muñeco means doll— or maybe "action hero" if you were trying to act tough. Tinker blinked and stayed silent, just as Marco expected him too. He was far too smart to offer an opinion.

Knox turned toward Marco and Tinker, then narrowed his eyes. "If you two tell anyone my real name..."

Rosita laughed. "He's named after our granddad."

Maite used the back of her hand to wipe mud off her mouth.

The knowledge of Knox's real name was going be a poker chip that Marco would hold onto for a very long time. But for now, he knew he had to clear the air with him.

"You did a really great job, Knox. Thanks for setting up the tech and the course and holding the mats and, really, for everything. I think you saved Growler's butt out there."

Growler turned on Marco's shoulder and shook his butt. Rosita answered the same way.

Knox nodded. "I had a job and wanted to keep on top of things." It wasn't a great apology, but it wasn't nothing neither.

"Okay," Maite said with an air of trying to break the tension. "Let's take down the electronics and get out of here. We don't want Old Man Jenkins finding a crowd."

Rosita, Maite, and Marco followed Tinker and Knox through the backlot to unrig cameras, roll cables, and monitors. Growler, Camo, Stinky, and Clank stayed back to "guard" the main console. It was a *very* important job, according to Tinker, so the monsters fanned out around the console, with Clank in the middle, to make sure nothing happened, as if anything would.

Between the five of them, it only took about ten minutes to take everything down. But in that time, Knox managed to sneak up next to Marco without him noticing, which was not something Marco would've been cool with at any other time.

"Marco, it was good that you apologized first. You were both wrong," he said, raising an eyebrow as if daring Marco to challenge him. Marco didn't. "But the important thing is *you* were wrong, and it didn't matter if Tink was too. *You* were. So since *you* were wrong, you needed to fix things cuz if you can't admit you're wrong, you don't *deserve* friends." Knox leaned in and got nose to nose with him. "And if my sister becomes *more* than a friend and starts hanging out with you more, and you wrong her, the murder and mayhem coming to you won't be cats."

Holy crayfish, Marco thought.

"But you proved yourself a bit today. Keep that up." He walked away.

Marco swallowed hard. He couldn't imagine what kind of bullying Knox could do if he really dedicated himself to it.

A thought pierced him. Didn't Knox see he was wrong to bully and not apologize for it? Or did he *not* apologize on purpose, to show Marco how it feels when you're wronged—and the wronger doesn't make it right?

Doesn't matter, he told himself. It seems he and Knox had moved beyond bad feelings. And Marco truly understood someone wanting to protect family. The Cariños were closer than any family he knew. He made a promise to himself right then and there. *I'll be a lot quicker from now on to apologize if I'm wrong. And hopefully I'll spot my mistakes before they blow up.*

"Done, Marco?" Maite called. Rosita stood beside her, wearing a cable like a necklace.

"Yup, coming," Marco called. Within minutes, everyone had loaded electronics into red wagons and were pulling them out of the junkyard.

"Hey, y'all wanna come over to my place?" Marco asked. "My folks will be really happy to see ya."

Tinker high-fived him. Maite and Rosita nodded yes. Knox shrugged. The monsters hooted and jumped from shoulder to shoulder like squirrels hopping across fences. Rosita squealed when they all landed on her simultaneously. Clank beeped from atop his wagon.

Marco looked up at the bright sky. This Saturday with friends felt like a new start, like he was finally kicking off the school year in the right way. "This'll be a monster of a year."

• • • ● ● • ● • • • •

In his room that night, after a full day playing with friends and after the maelstrom of a bath with cannonballing monsters, Marco pulled out his photo with Tinker, both pieces of it, and some art supplies. Camo, Stinky, and Growler looked from the photo remnants to his face before nodding and crawling into bed.

Marco frowned at the tear. He'd never done photo restoration before, but he always felt his best approach to art was to learn by doing. He set the two halves of the photo face down on the nightstand and pressed some clear tape across the rip. He flipped the newly attached pieces over, and they mostly held, but the tear was still way too visible. He folded the halves back again, just enough to reopen the crease, and dropped a thin line of glue across it. After he flattened the photo again, this time face up, he ran a straight-edged ruler across to the crease to push off any raised glue. Finally, he used paint to touch up the division. It became nearly invisible, almost like there was never a rip, like nothing happened. Marco pondered seeing himself and Tinker frozen in time, laughing and smiling, arms draped over each others' shoulders. *Just like today*. It felt right.

"Me glad you and Tinky friends," Stinky said.

"Me too." Marco pulled the covers up to the chins of the monsters beside him, tucking them in. "Thanks, colegas, for everything."

Camo transformed to a field of stars. Growler snored.

Marco slid open the lower drawer of his nightstand and retrieved an empty picture frame. He slid the photo in and showed Stinky and Camo, who grinned sleepily and closed their eyes.

Marco set the picture frame on his nightstand, his place of honor, where he kept his favorite things to look at before bed. His bestie definitely belonged there.

Marco turned off the lamp, maneuvered himself onto the crowded bed, and closed his eyes. He imagined how tomorrow might go, taking his monsters over to Tink's. He had nearly drifted to sleep when he heard his phone buzz. He had plugged it back in after his bath, ready to hear from friends again. He opened his nightstand drawer and fished it out. He saw a text bubble from Tink.

> you know clank crossed the finish line first right

>> nuh uh growler beat him by a mile

> we'll check the video tomorrow lol

>> haha ok, yum it's pancakes sunday

> yep, and you and your monsters can try out my new hoverboard, it really hovers

>> whoa that's amazing can't wait to try it

> and we can paint too, maybe give Clank some racing stripes

> sounds fun see you tomorrow :-)

> :-) :-) :-)

Marco laughed, put his phone away, and rolled toward his monsters. They were cozied up and warm, peaceful as could be. Marco closed his eyes and joined them.

Please leave a review

Three Points Publishing depends on word of mouth for its success. If you enjoyed this book, please help others learn about it by leaving a review on your favorite bookish site. Thank you!

Book Reflection Guide

We hope you enjoyed reading *Mail-Order Monsters: Crash Course*. We've added these questions to encourage discussion and deeper thinking about the story. The questions have SPOILERS, so you may want to read the story before looking at these questions.

1. Do you think Marco believed the monsters would be real when he cut the ad out of the comic book? Why did he want them? Why would we sometimes want believe in magic rather than face difficulties? Would you have done the same as Marco?

2. In art class, Marco imagines himself as a dragon who could intimidate Knox. Have you ever imagined yourself intimidating a bully or rival? How did that make you feel? Did it boost Marco's confidence? When Marco's pushed, Tinker saves his mask from

destruction. What does that say about Tink?

3. At lunch, Marco eats at the same table as Tinker and the Cariños. Why doesn't he or Tinker leave for another table? When Rosita tries to melt lunchroom iciness by telling jokes, Knox tells her to stop trying to bring together people who don't belong together. Do you agree with Marco that the comment is mean? Or do you think Knox is right?

4. When Marco talks to his monsters in the bathtub, we get a better picture of the kids' relationships toward each other. Was Tinker justified in being angry? Is Marco right to be angry right back? Can you guess yet why Knox feels justified in bullying Marco, even though bullying is wrong? Describe the relationship dynamics between the Cariño siblings.

5. Marco's crushing on Maite but doesn't really know what that means. Have you ever faced a situation where you haven't really understood what's happening or how to get through it? How did you help yourself?

6. After his bathtub confession, Marco wonders if anyone is as honest with another per-

son as he was with his monsters. Do you think everyone has a secret? Who might you trust with yours? Is it okay to not share secrets?

7. That night, Marco worries about the final part of the directions, to have faith. Why might that be hard for him?

8. Marco is happiest when he's creating art. It's part of who he is. Tinker loves mechanics and engineering. Do you have a special talent or one you wish you had? How does Marco's desire to start an art club demonstrate his devotion to developing his craft?

9. Discuss Marco's relationship with his parents.

10. Why did Maite visit Marco at home? Is her influence on him positive or negative?

11. When Marco brought the monsters to school, he got the huge reaction he'd hoped for, except from people who thought the monsters might be pets. Are Growler, Stinky, and Camo like pets? Or are they more like people? Which monster friend is your favorite?

12. How do most people behave around Marco once they learn he has monsters?

13. Marco leaves his usual lunch table so he can feed his monsters hiding under the stage. In what way does his move show his allegiance to his monster friends over his human friends?

14. In their race training, the monsters show great friendship and camaraderie. In what ways does their example influence Marco?

15. Tinker creates a robot that can drive, technology which has just recently come into being in the form of "self-driving" cars. Yet Tinker's friends have no trouble believing he could create such tech. What does that say about his reputation?

16. Rosita is nervous before the race. However, once she starts her play-by-play announcing, she's confident and does an excellent job. Maite says it's because she practiced before the event. Have you ever practiced something enough that you were surprised how well you did?

17. Knox is named after his granddad, Muñeco,

and tries to hide that name. Would you do the same? Should he instead be proud of it?

18. Do you think Knox was hypocritical when he told Marco to apologize sooner if he's at fault for something regardless if someone else is also at fault? Do you think maybe he didn't apologize himself because he wants Marco to know what it feels like? Or do you think Knox doesn't see it?

19. At the end of the novel, Marco and Tinker joke about who won the race. Why does or doesn't this matter?

20. Stinky says, "Me glad you and Tinky friends." How does that reflect on the monsters?

21. Friendship is a major theme in the novel. Describe what makes a good friend. How have you been a good friend? Where have you fallen short? How do the characters' friendships evolve throughout the story?

22. Humor plays a big role in this novel too. Which are your favorite funny moments? You favorite funny lines? The author likes these best: * *Their friendship was unraveling like frayed rope.* * *Once a teacher thinks*

*you're a bad egg, you're cooked. * Word of the race spread through school like germs in play-dough.*

23. Look closely at the illustrations. How do they capture the fun and emotion of the story? Why do you think the book ends with a drawing? Would Marco approve?

24. Spanish words and phrases are sprinkled throughout the book. The author sometimes translates these phrases directly and sometimes uses context to explain their meaning. Why do you think the author didn't include a glossary in this book?

25. The monsters' magic brings them to life, but humans have a kind of magic too—concern for one another. Give examples of when characters showed heartfelt concern toward each other.

Acknowledgements

This book took more years, work, and cheerleading than I ever expected, but all that made the story better. I sincerely hope you loved it.

A dazzling group of fabulous people helped this project see the light of day. First and foremost, I thank my husband for his love, support, and *gestures wildly* *everything*ness. I simply wouldn't be where I am without his deep belief in me and sheer will to make things happen. Thanks, Jeff, for seeing this through and adding adventure at every turn. You get a zillion husband points and even more gold stars. Reader, if you liked the illustrations throughout this story, you too can thank Jeff, as he is the illustrator of the cover and interior art. Jeff even came up with the original idea for this story, so Mail-Order Monsters is as much his as mine.

My next biggest heap of thanks and praise goes to my closest writing pal and fiercest critique partner, Valerie Biel. Val is an accomplished author in her own right and helped add to the monster hijinks. Importantly, she encouraged me during the many obstacles and dips in my publishing journey. I'm deeply grateful for our friendship. Fellow critiquers Keith Pitsch, Christine Keleny, and Dave Emanuel (may he rest in peace) are powerhouses who pointed out what worked, what didn't, and suggested new paths forward.

Other writers who rallied around me and continue to make the creative life fun include author and former school teacher Christy Wopat, who answered my school-related questions and is simply a dynamo in her own right. Thanks also to Kristin Oakley, Rebecca Hirsch, Kerry Hanen, Liza Wiemer, Tracy S. Phillips, Pat Zietlow Miller, and Laurie Scheer, all fellow or former Wisconsin writers, for reading various versions and/or cheerleading throughout. Michelle Houts's insights prompted me to analyze and dissect my reasoning.

I'd like to recognize the Society of Children's Book Writers and Illustrators for educating a newbie novelist over the years and for bestowing this story with not one but TWO awards: the Work of Outstanding Progress honor award and a regional Most Promising Manuscript award. These pats on the back propel a writer like you wouldn't believe. Thanks also to the Wisconsin Writers Association for allowing me to share my publishing know-how with members and for championing writers everywhere.

My (now grown) children have seen countless iterations of *Mail-Order Monsters*. Endless thanks, kids, for your insight, suggestions, and love. This story is finally out in the world! Yaaaaay! May the next generation lose themselves in it as you once did.

I salute you, dear reader, for investing your time with this story. I'm honored you chose to do so.

To comic book shops everywhere, thanks for giving little kids (and us big kids) a landing pad to flip through piles of comics filled with exciting adventures and, of course, the occasional ad for monster friends. Stinky would no doubt dive into every comic book bin just to get that musty comic smell all over him.

To all the little monsters out there, whether hiding under beds, in closets, or crawling through school air ducts, I can assure you that none of your brethren were harmed in the making of this book.

Now, everyone, go forth and be monstrous.

About the author

Silvia Acevedo is an award-winning children's book author who also runs a workshop for artists. Before writing about made-up worlds, she stuck to the facts as a reporter and anchor for TV, radio, magazines, and newspapers. She is the human companion to a varying number of cats, two of whom are depicted in this story as Murder and Mayhem and who are, without a doubt, simply *meow*velous.

About the artist

Jeff Miracola's been making fantasy art since 1993 for cool projects like Star Wars, Mars Attacks, Dungeons & Dragons, and World of Warcraft. He's most known, though, for his 30+ years creating art for Magic: The Gathering. He's also done conceptual toy and video game design, editorial illustrations, and picture books, as well as activity books for Klutz/Scholastic. Jeff's a sucker for animals, so when he's not creating art, he's feeding his many cats and befriending all the squirrels, chipmunks, and birds that swoop his way.

Look for Book 2 in the Mail-Order Monsters series

Marco and friends have more monstrous fun in Book 2 of the Mail-Order Monster series, coming soon.

Also by Silvia Acevedo

THE HAUNTED STATES OF AMERICA
"Shiver your way across the United States of fear in this collection of paranormal stories by a diverse range of authors...An entertaining, fright-filled geographical tour."—Kirkus Reviews

The GOD AWFUL trilogy
GOD AWFUL LOSER; GOD AWFUL THIEF; and *GOD AWFUL REBEL,* WINNER of the Society of Children's Book Writers and Illustrators's SPARK AWARD for excellence

www.ingramcontent.com/pod-product-compliance
Lightning Source LLC
LaVergne TN
LVHW091416180825
818734LV00001B/5